The Destroyer

151: BULLY PULPIT

WARREN MURPHY WITH R.J. CARTER

DESTROYER BOOKS
© WARREN MURPHY MEDIA

This is a work of fiction. All the characters and events portrayed in this book are fictional, and any resemblance to real people or real incidents is purely coincidental.

THE DESTROYER #151: BULLY PULPIT

COPYRIGHT © 2016 WARREN MURPHY MEDIA, LLC

All rights reserved, including the right to reproduce this book or any portion thereof, in any form or in any manner, except for reviews or commentary.

This edition published in 2016 by Warren Murphy Media
E-book edition published in 2016 by Gere Donovan Press

ISBN-13: 978-1-944073-69-5 (Destroyer Books)
ISBN-10: 1-944073-69-8

Requests for reproduction or interviews should be directed to
DestroyerBooks@gmail.com

Cover art by Gere Donovan Press/Devin Murphy

In Memoriam: Warren Murphy
September 13, 1933 – September 4, 2015
The Master has put down his pen. May his words live on.

To Jeffery O'Neill Lynch,
whom I've never met.
But he introduced Remo to Keith Sweet,
who introduced him to me.

— R.J. Carter

CHAPTER ONE

Nobody walks in los angeles. If Jacob Riser had been walking, he would have looked suspicious. But Jacob Riser was not walking. He was running, which was a certified heart-healthy activity, and was therefore perfectly acceptable—as well as eminently ignorable—even at three in the morning.

Jacob's lungs burned as he gasped for air in the oxygen-deficient atmosphere of the big city. It might have gone easier for Jacob if he'd done more running in his life, but it had been twenty years and several thousand cigarettes since his last sprint.

Most people ran because they wanted to live longer, and that was certainly true in Jacob's case as he rounded a corner blindly, his second-hand Florsheims desperate to find traction on the concrete.

Several yards into a narrow alleyway, Jacob squatted behind a dumpster, willing his heart to slow, his wheezing to silence. He glanced at the opening to the alley through a narrow aperture afforded between the back of the dumpster and the brick wall it abutted.

As he began to let himself believe he had escaped, that his pursuer had been evaded, he opened once more the manila folder he had been clutching to his chest. It was proof—*proof*, damn it!—that he was right this time, that he'd finally pegged that bastard after so many mistakes. But, oh God, how could the man be this evil? He had to be insane. There was no explanation, no reason, no *profit* in this. It staggered the mind.

Fingers shaking, Jacob fumbled in his jacket pocket for his cell phone, thumbing through the directory for the first person he thought might listen to him.

The sound of the phone warbling on the other end echoed like a klaxon in the alleyway, and Jacob quickly cupped his hand over the speaker, his heart swelling up into his throat.

A dozen rings later, an older and decidedly crabby voice came on the line. "Who the hell is this and why the holy hell are you calling me at the ass crack of dawn?"

"Schultzie," Jacob whispered into the phone. "Schultzie, it's me. It's Jake. From *The Clarion*. Remember?"

"Jake?" There was a groan in his voice that said Schultzie would have much rather been awakened by a telephone solicitor. "Aw, holy cripes, Riser, is that you? I thought you were out west stalking celebutantes for crotch shots."

"Schultzie, listen," Jake persisted. "I got him. I finally got that son of a bitch."

There was a long pause on the other end of the phone. "Jake, if you got me up just to give me another cockamamie conspiracy on…"

"This is real, Schultzie! It's unbelievable, but..."

"Yeah, well, after the last time that doesn't really surprise me."

Jacob closed his eyes and took a breath. "Okay. Okay, I deserve that. But listen..."

"No. No, you listen, Jake," Schultzie interrupted. "I stood up for you last time. I put my friggin' reputation on the line, you remember that? I stood up and I told that editorial board, 'Jake's a decent guy and a hard working reporter. If he says there's monkey business going on, then by God you better believe there's monkey business going on.' I pushed for you!"

"I...I remember, Schultzie."

"I was lucky—*damn* lucky—that they didn't shitcan me when it all hit the fan. *Damn* lucky they didn't decide to include me in that lawsuit, though they might as well have. I've been paying for your screw up ever since! You've been a shit stain I can't wash out."

"Schultzie," Jacob pleaded. "This isn't like that! I swear."

"Jake, honest to God, I don't care if you have pictures of him in bed with farm animals. You burned me once. You're not going to do it again. Call someone else."

"There isn't..." The phone showed the call had terminated. "...anyone else," Jacob finished weakly to the dead connection.

He slipped the phone back into his pocket. He'd stayed in one place too long already. He needed to keep moving. With complaints from both knees and a sharp stitch in his side,

Jacob pulled himself into a standing position, just in time to see his pursuer standing silhouetted against the streetlight at the opening of the alley.

Jacob wheeled and sprinted down the alley, wheezing as every fiber of his being struggled for survival. He'd gone about twenty paces when the bullet cut through his lower spine and burst out his gut. His legs lost all the signals from the rest of his central nervous system, and inertia face-planted him into the pavement with all the mercy gravity could muster, which was none. The cartilage of his nose popped like a balloon filled with raspberry jelly.

Jacob lay there, unable to move, unable to see beyond the fireworks on the back of his eyelids. He heard the unhurried, measured footsteps of his killer approaching, heard the click of the .38 snub-nosed revolver's hammer being pulled back, and heard the pop of the bullet leaving the barrel as his body jerked once more. Each labored breath expulsed thick, viscous fluid now, and every nerve in his body screamed in pain.

He felt the manila folder pulled free from beneath his body as his killer tugged at an exposed corner. If Jacob had it in him to care at that moment, he would have pondered how his impending death was only going to be the insignificant first of so many, many more, and not long from now.

"*Alas! for that day is great, so that none is like it: it is even the time of Jacob's trouble; but he shall be saved out of it.*" His killer's voice was soft but sonorous, practiced from years of public oratory. "And another prophecy is thus fulfilled. I thank you for that, Mister Riser."

BULLY PULPIT

Jacob burbled as he felt a hand slip into his back pocket and pull out his billfold. His killer availed himself of the forty-two dollars inside, letting the emptied soft leather fall conspicuously to the ground beside Jacob's prone body before walking calmly away.

A short distance away, he heard a female voice. "We would have done that for you, honey," the voice said. "It would have been faster."

"I couldn't let you do that," the killer said ruefully. "My soul's already damned. I don't have the right to condemn yours."

Five minutes later and three blocks north, a homeless man with a sign declaring he could not find a job, an education, or a meal, yet who had no difficulty in locating a clean piece of cardboard and a magic marker, found himself suddenly blessed with two twenties and two singles, and readied himself for a breakfast of liquid gold.

As Jacob's mind began to shut down, his fingers reached outward, grasping for the cement foundation of the wall beside him. His fingers slick with blood, he had neither the time nor the cognition to leave a detailed message, or even a name, for whoever would find his body. Instead, he painted the last solid fact he could focus on, the single-most important thing he had ever learned: 1:49. And then his arm fell, as Jacob's last breath rattled past his lips, blowing one final bubble of blood.

But who could decipher the meaning of the numbers in time? Who could possibly stop the coming apocalypse?

CHAPTER TWO

HIS NAME WAS REMO, AND HE THOUGHT he had sworn off smoking forever.

He was ambling along a crowded sidewalk. It was quiet, eerily calm, as he passed storefronts boarded up the way he had seen businesses do in advance of a hurricane. But there was no hurricane bearing down on Archway City, which was a thousand miles from any coast. It was something worse: a mood, a hive mind mentality that created a tension that was almost tangible. There were several police on hand, but they were all barricaded in their vehicles. Remo tapped on one of the patrol car windows, and an officer rolled it down an inch.

"Yeah, what do you want?"

Remo put his palms up, keeping them in plain sight so the officer would feel there wasn't a threat. "Just wanted to get a sitrep."

"Sitrep?" the officer asked. "Oh, the situation. Nothing confirmed yet, but word is the grand jury is going to announce any minute. And if it goes the way I'm hearing, you might want to get inside where it's safe."

"Think it's going to get that bad, huh?"

"Worse," the officer replied.

Remo looked around. "So where are you guys hiding the riot gear, or the paddy wagons for all the arrests?"

"Arrests?" the officer laughed. "There won't be any arrests. We've got orders to stand down and let the citizens express themselves. Any action on our part will be interpreted as an abridgment of their First Amendment rights to free speech."

The Constitution wasn't something the officer had to explain to Remo. He'd been defending it for some time now—usually by violating it. In what had seemed a simpler time, Remo had been a beat cop himself, back in Newark. Then one day he blinked, and found himself in prison on a trumped up charge that landed him on death row. As his fellow inmates served out decades, living on appeal after appeal, Remo was sent to the electric chair, where he was summarily executed.

Instead of awakening to Saint Peter and sweet angel harps, Remo woke up in a hospital bed from a medically induced coma to the irritating shrill insults of an ancient Korean. He learned from a dour man named Harold W. Smith that his identity had been eradicated so that he could serve as the enforcement arm of CURE, an agency created by the past President to exist outside of the Constitution in order to defend it in ways that it couldn't do itself. To do this, he would be trained by Master

Chiun, the Korean whom he was sure hated him for no good reason at the time, in the assassin's art of Sinanju. And, for the good of the United States of America, Remo had accepted the offer.

Since that time, he had encountered a number of weird and unbelievable atrocities, but few of them ever topped human nature at its pure nastiest.

• • •

Downtown, several miles from Remo, a battalion of media cameras and reporters were gathered on the steps of the courthouse. At this very moment, as the last sliver of sunlight slunk behind the western horizon, the special prosecutor was about to announce to the world that the grand jury had found no credible evidence to indict Officer Eric Ritter in the shooting death of eighteen-year-old Demond Wilcox. Despite the distance, those comments sparked a fuse that sizzled at the speed of social media, making a beeline for the northeast suburban neighborhood, almost directly to the mound of dead flowers, candles, and a rain-matted teddy bear—centrally laid out around a 40 ounce bottle of beer, marking the spot in the street where Wilcox breathed his last.

The fuse may not have been real, but the explosions were—very real. A shouting, angry mob appeared nearly spontaneously. The police officer Remo was talking to rolled up his window, and the rest obeyed their orders and sheltered in place while the protestors threw bottles, broke windows, flipped cars and chanted bad poetry at the top of their lungs.

The first building went up in flames within minutes, a bakery owned by an old man who gave out free cupcakes to the neighborhood children who came in on their birthdays. Remo stood on a corner against a light pole, disappointed that humanity didn't disappoint him, as he watched the flames climb higher into the sky. The absence of sirens told him nobody was coming to save this structure, and the absence of screaming told him there was nobody inside—this time.

Remo glanced up and down the street, counting heads and giving a low whistle. It was painfully obvious that there were more people charging about than made up the population of the neighborhood.

This wasn't protesting authority, Remo realized. Protesting authority was the sperm and egg of America. This was madness—with coordination.

He let out a deep sigh, and then tilted his head slightly to the right to allow a bottle of what Remo hoped was lemonade sail past him to smash on the sidewalk further away. The immediate ammonia and asparagus smell emanating from the bottle's impact evaporated any hopes Remo had that it was merely a waste of a refreshing fruit drink. He turned, and saw even more insanity going on down the street behind him, with multiple plumes of smoke making columns against the blackening sky.

Across the street, Roland Perry was putting a flame to the t-shirt wick of his Molotov cocktail, before sending it in a high arc against the plywood planks boarding up the windows of the 24 hour Git-It-N-Go, which was closed for the first time in its thirty years in the neighborhood.

"How's it going?" Remo asked amiably, startling Perry who hadn't heard Remo slip up on him.

"Burn this mother down!" he shouted by way of response.

"Okay, but why?"

Roland Perry looked him up and down, taken off guard by this ignorant fool who didn't seem to be getting into the spirit of the protest. He wore a dressy pair of chinos, which screamed military—maybe a National Guard soldier, but they were supposed to be across town—and his forearms, which were crossed loosely over his chest, seemed to disappear into his hands without bothering to taper into wrists. Despite the unassuming tone of his voice, the dark eyes shadowed by his pronounced brow communicated anything but friendliness.

"Why?" Roland repeated dumbly. "*Why?* Because these are *our* streets! This is *our* neighborhood!"

"So where do you plan to live tomorrow?"

"Where…?"

"Where are you going to get gas? Where are you going to buy cupcakes? You might have a few holdout heroin dealers, but the smarter ones are already on their way to safer pastures."

BULLY PULPIT

The flames were licking higher up the side of the Git-It-N-Go, the plywood letting loose of the building, the plate glass shattering from the heat.

The destruction bolstered Roland's courage. "Why you giving me shit?" he asked indignantly. "You ain't from around here. These are *our* streets! This is…"

"I know, I know." Remo repeated. "'This is our neighborhood.'" He sighed. "Tell you what, let's take a walk, you and me."

"Take a what?" But Roland was already moving, as Remo's hand appeared almost magically beside Roland's head, thumb and forefinger pinching a rather sensitive nerve cluster in his upper earlobe. "Ow! Ow! Hey, where we goin'?"

Inside the Git-It-N-Go, the flames were licking at the racks of cheese puffs and snack cakes, toxic plastic wrappers melting and molding to their contents, which didn't cause the food-like substances to be any more toxic than they already were.

"What the hell, man," shrieked a panicked Roland Perry, as Remo led him by the ear into the centermost area of the convenience store. "Are you out of your mind? Leggo my ear, you crazy cracker!"

"Sure thing," Remo said cheerfully. "Soon as you show me where the sunflower seeds are."

"The sunflower…what?" Roland's eyes were wide with fear, and his face was a sheen of sweat. "Man, this place is gonna come down around us!"

"Then we should probably hurry," Remo said. Roland noted that the heat wasn't affecting his abuser—even his pants weren't getting singed, as Roland frantically slapped away a few sparks from his gravity-defying droopy drawers. "I'd never find them on my own. Good thing you're from the neighborhood, Roland."

"Dude, we have got to...Ow! That's my ear, man!"

"You have two ears, Roland," Remo said. "When you have two of something, and you use neither, you can't miss one if it's gone."

A wall of flame grew rapidly up the counter, strings of scratch off tickets curling, smoldering, and ultimately igniting with enough heat to crack the glass case. Roland squealed, then began to look hurriedly for sunflower seeds. He saw a row of candy bars that hadn't attracted flames yet. "Over there! They're over there!" he pointed.

Remo looked where Roland was pointing. "Are you sure, Roland? I'd hate to go on a wild goose chase. You know, what with the building burning down and all." He tugged Roland's ear, leading him in the general direction of the candy bars. "I'm not seeing them, Roland."

"They're here, they gotta be," Roland said. He was starting to cough, and yet this crazy mother was still as calm and cool as if he were browsing a farmer's market. He began to rake through the different boxes of chocolates and peanuts, spilling them to the floor.

"I thought this was your neighborhood, Roland?" Remo teased. "Maybe the store remodeled since you were here last?"

"Man, I don't..." It was then that realization managed to wedge its way through a crack in Roland's terror. "Hey, how you know my name, man? I didn't tell you my name!"

"I'm impressed, Roland," Remo said. "Maybe your ears are starting to get some use after all." His other hand came into view. It was holding a wallet—specifically Roland's. He let the wallet fall open. "Roland Perry, 344 Clinton Street...Oh, this can't be right. This says Chicago on it. You know you're supposed to change your license when you move, don't you Roland?"

"Man, how you get my wallet?"

"Well, I have to tell you, you did make it a challenge," Remo chuckled. "I mean, lifting a wallet, that's almost child's play. But the real trick was to get it out of your back pocket without knocking your pants to the ground. That, I don't mind saying, took a little bit of finesse. But more to the point, what are you doing in Archway City? Because I think we've pretty much established that these are *not* your streets and this is *not* your neighborhood."

"I ain't gotta tell you sh—" The tempered glass doors of the freezer shattered loudly, sending shards flying out and catching him across the face. When he looked back up, the man with his wallet didn't have a scratch on him.

"Better hurry, Roland," Remo said. "Things are starting to heat up."

Blood ran into Roland's right eye, stinging it, and the smoke was getting thicker. "A'right, a'right! We took buses, okay? We all got in last week."

"Oh, I'm going to need a few more details than that, Roland," Remo said calmly, as a rack of Flaming Hot potato chips ignited and crashed to the ground at the end of the aisle. "Who's 'we,' for instance?"

"I don't know, man!" Roland tried to yank his head away from Remo's grip, and his vision went white with pain. "Leggo me, man!" he screamed in agony.

"But you haven't found my sunflower seeds yet, Roland," Remo said. "I'll forgive you that if you tell me who came on the buses."

"Seriously, I don't know," Roland whimpered. "We didn't know each other. We just got word that the Reverend Bluntman..."

"Wait, Hal Bluntman?"

"Yeah, Reverend Hal, he put out the word that we was gonna teach this town a lesson. But that's all I know man, I swear!"

Remo sighed. "Okay, I believe you, Roland." He let go of the man's ear. "Now get out of here. Go make something positive out of your life. Because if I see you again at another..."

Remo paused. His feet felt the pressure waves gently ripple under the floor of the convenience store. The sensation was imperceptible to anyone else, but that would soon change. Remo felt his stomach go a little queasy, like when he used to ride the tilt-a-whirl as a kid back on the boardwalk.

Roland Perry wasn't going to ask questions. Seeing

BULLY PULPIT

Remo's attention had shifted to other things, he turned and bolted toward the door—only he didn't know which way the door was now, since the building had filled with flames and smoke. He pivoted one direction, then the other.

And that's when Roland became aware of what Remo already knew was coming, as the ground rumbled fiercely, upending one wall of the store while lowering another. With provident accuracy, one of the roof beams of the already weakened structure fell, its flaming mass striking Roland squarely in the head, caving in the side of his skull and knocking him to the ground.

"Well, hell," Remo muttered, as he stepped lightly across the flaming wreckage. "Really didn't mean for that to happen, Roland," he offered in apology, as he stepped through the door, unharmed and into the night where chaos continued to reign up and down the street.

As he took in the scene of rampaging citizens and cowering cops, he smelled something burning that was different from all the other things that were burning. Looking down at his arm, he saw that the tips of a few hairs were glowing embers, sending up tiny, curling wisps of smoke. His already-low brow ridge lowered further as Remo cursed himself mentally. "Clumsy," he muttered, brushing the embers out with one sweep of his palm. "Thank God Chiun wasn't here to see that."

• • •

When Remo made it back downtown to the justice

building, walking past several idle National Guard troops protecting the expensive property from protests that weren't happening, he found Chiun sitting beatifically on the top step of the courthouse, arms folded and eyes closed. He had felt no need to follow Remo into what he poetically called "the jungle." Besides, the pool of reporters swarming the scene earlier would include the illustrious Cheeta Ching, who was, according to Chiun, the only newscaster worth watching because her beauty distracted from the pitiful quality of the information she was imparting.

"You were right Chiun," Remo said, disgustedly. "They're animals."

"Say that first part again," Chiun replied, not opening his eyes. "These ears are old, and frequently lie to me."

Remo sat beside him. "I said you were right, Little Father," he replied. "As always. At least I got a name for Smitty."

"A pitiful use of Sinanju," Chiun said, the vellum slits of his eyelids cracking open just the tiniest bit. "Nothing of value came from this needless trip."

"Cheeta Ching didn't even notice you, huh?"

"Oh, she was here?" Chiun asked, unperturbed. "I did not notice."

"She was three feet from where you're sitting, Chiun," Remo grinned. "You were practically looking up her—"

"We should go now," Chiun said, rising to his feet, "before you finish uttering a slander against one who has only ever put you before all other matters in his life."

Remo smiled to himself, ready with a rejoinder, when he thought he noticed Chiun slightly stumble as he rose. Before he could reach out to right his Master, Chiun had recovered, as though it had never happened.

"Chiun, are you—" He was interrupted by the chirping of the phone in his pants pocket.

"It is the bird in the box again," Chiun said. "Why do you not free yourself of it?"

"Smitty said we're supposed to slide it left when it rings," Remo said, as he swiped the phone in a leftward motion along his arm.

Chiun rolled his eyes. "Not like that, let me—"

"I've got it, Little Father."

"Why does the mad Emperor Smith not send an envoy?" Chiun grumbled. "That would be more dignified for a Master of Sinanju."

• • •

In a remote, pastoral corner of Westchester County, looking out over the Long Island Sound, is a facility for housing and treating those who struggle with reality. The old timers in the area still used the term 'sanitarium' (with the really old timers calling it 'the bughouse'), and indeed Folcroft Sanitarium hadn't bothered to change its name for years, despite evolutions in polite language.

Now and again, you might catch a smirk from a few smartly-dressed employees having lunch at Ruby's Oyster Bar & Bistro when asked how things were going out at the 'hospital.' These were the guys who knew that Folcroft Sanitarium was no mere rest home, but was in fact a cover for the National Security Administration's top-secret software development laboratories. Certainly, it housed a great number of mentally ill, employed a platoon of nurses, and a team of the best doctors—as well as one cold-hearted administrator who everyone was fairly sure popped out of the womb with his lips pursed like he'd sucked on his first lemon.

It was the computer systems inside Folcroft that were the real reason for its existence—systems that played host to sophisticated, real-time data analysis software that would, in a few years or so, be the next level of cutting-edge technology for keeping the United States safe. Before that happened, however, it would serve as the *bleeding* edge analysis tool for what was actually the most secretive agency in America—so secretive that even the employees didn't realize who employed them.

Folcroft's chief of staff provided the perfect cover for the development project; the doctor was gray, boring, and showed an absolute void of curiosity. Even his name embodied an aura of bland homogeneity: Smith.

Harold W. Smith was also the head of CURE—was, in fact, one-half of the total organization, and one of only three people who knew of the organization's existence. Every day, Smith would enter his drab office, hang his gray overcoat and hat, straighten his tie and adjust his

American flag lapel pin, then sit down before the CURE computer monitor where he would begin to purse his lips even tighter as statistics and probabilities began to dance across the glass. The system monitored global events in real time, connecting the dots and stringing together links that, to human beings, would appear superficially disparate. These clusters of data floated on a rotating three-dimensional wireframe model. Items the computer deemed more important than others were displayed in glowing red letters.

Smith had long ago learned to trust the machine. But he also subscribed to the philosophy of one of the Presidents he had had the privilege to serve under: Trust, but verify.

Several events vied for his attention. Civil unrest in the Midwest threatened to escalate. Small, scattered groups in Texas were determined to press the issue of making assault rifles and grenade launchers as common a sight as backpacks and purses in preschools and grocery stores. Smith touched the screen and brushed each of these clusters aside for later scrutiny.

In prominent, thick letters, the CURE system insisted Smith give attention to the increase in global earthquake activity. Smith's eyebrows scrunched together, and his lemony face puckered as he puzzled over this bit of information. The earthquakes weren't focused in any one area, and he ultimately decided there was nothing to be done with this. He then pushed the dataset over into the digital wastebasket, making a note for future upgrades to place less weight on natural disasters.

This manual bit of cleanup made the next warning one Smith was more comfortable in handling: a third-tier terrorist organization, ya Homaar, had been on CURE's radar for some time now, having displayed a spark of potential at evolving into the next Daesh or ibn Kalaab. What had been holding them back had been their lack of funding, yet the chatter stitched together by CURE's Internet sniffers gave all indications that, even without money, the group had come into possession of several explosive devices which they were looking to put to use soon. Smith double-tapped the image of the data cluster, which began to unfold onto the screen, extrapolating the sequence of comments as the machine's predictive engines began extrapolating likely targets and assessing threat levels.

Satisfied with the 98% probability factors, Smith picked up the phone—an archaic black rotary device—out of place in any other office but which fit right in with the timeless spartan decor of Smith's domain. The phone ever only dialed one number, and only ever rang from two, so there was no need for it to have any other features.

Without needing to dial, Smith heard a connection begin to ring on the other end. After what had become the customary thirty rings, the connection was opened and he heard two voices arguing for several moments before he was finally able to speak.

"Smitty," Remo's voice came through the receiver. "You called this one. Someone's definitely orchestrating these riots. I got one of them to pony up Hal Bluntman's name. You want the usual?"

"We'll have to table that for now," Smith replied curtly. "For now, go to the airport. Your tickets will be waiting."

CHAPTER THREE

IN THE BACK OF A CAVE, halfway up a mountain populated by a small herd of nervous, skittish goats, a man hunched over a keyboard, then muttered a curse.

"The Wi-Fi reception out here is horrible," he complained in Arabic, thumping the side of a monitor. "Why can we not have a nice compound like Daesh?" he asked his companion, Akbar, who was just entering the mouth of the cave.

"Because of money, Achmed," the other man replied. "But our day is coming, my brother. Be patient."

"I think I shall die of patience," said Achmed. "Who do we have to kill to get a little cash flow going?"

Akbar smiled. "I have good news about that," he said, patting Achmed on the shoulder. "The lunatic infidel proselytizer, who knows not Allah, has made good on his offer, and has sent us a great gift."

"Money?" the seated terrorist asked hopefully.

"Better, my brother. Better. He has gifted us with bombs."

"Oh," said Achmed, visibly crestfallen.

"Even now our brethren are..." The sound of an explosion burst through the cave, interrupting him and causing him to leap behind an outcropping of stone, one foot landing in a goat patty as he did so.

"Ah! My connection is back up," Achmed exclaimed gleefully. "Oh, damn it to hell, he killed me."

"Achmed, what are you doing?" Akbar asked, scraping his sandal against the wall to remove the bulk of the goat dung.

"I am trying to demoralize the forces of the Great Satan by proving our superior combat skills to them through their electronic war games."

"And are you succeeding?"

He sighed. "Not yet, Akbar. But I will."

"All things with time, my brother," Akbar encouraged.

"You've been toasted, brah!" an electronic voice warbled from the computer's speakers, as the twelve-year-old on the other end gloated. Achmed cursed again and smacked the keyboard. "Soon you will die," he muttered.

"Soon indeed," Akbar said. "For as I was telling you, even now our brethren are on their way to make known to all the fearsome name of ya Homaar. They have one of the infidel's bombs with them."

Achmed looked up with ardent glee. "And where shall they make this statement, oh my brother? Washington? London? Tokyo?"

Akbar grinned.

"Jersey."

CHAPTER FOUR

THE LOOSENESS OF THE YELLOW SILK KIMONO with the gold brocade hid that Chiun was sitting lotus position on the large flat rock as he looked out toward the sea. To his left lay a chaotic smattering of lottery tickets, their silver painted squares unmarred as the piled up in the sand. To his right, stacked neatly, were winning tickets ready to be cashed in. A light breeze blew in off the water as Chiun, eyes closed, passed his palm over another ticket.

"A-ha!" he cried. "Another worthless piece of paper." He discarded the ticket, letting it litter the sand beside him with its other untouched brethren. "Why do you not buy just the tickets that are worth more money?" he asked Remo.

"Because, Little Father, that would be considered stealing," Remo explained patiently as Chiun slowly slid his palm over another ticket. He had checked into the Grand Merlot Valeton hotel under the name Remo Robespierre, then picked up a newspaper at the gift shop, which was where Chiun found the roll of scratch off tickets and insisted Remo buy the entire set.

"They charged you a fee for their goods, and you paid it,

did you not? Is it stealing when they say they are giving you money and you gratefully accept it?" Chiun asked. "If they were *not* giving the money away, then that would be stealing."

"They're not giving it away, Chiun," Remo said. "There's a risk that you won't win. That's supposed to be the thrill of gambling, the idea that you might lose your money."

"There is no risk," Chiun said serenely in his chiding, sing-song cadence. He lay the current ticket carefully on the stack, having scratched off only the three matching squares indicating a 5 Euro win. "There is money, and there is no money. The wise Master of Sinanju chooses the path leading where there is money." He opened his eyes and glanced out at the ocean as if just noticing it. "This is a nicer place than you usually take me, Remo. Why have you avoided this place before?"

"Because this isn't Jersey in the US of A, it's Jersey off the coast of France," Remo said. The newspaper he was flipping through made no mention of the peace talks currently underway between representatives of the Palestinians and Israelis, due to the fact that the talks were supposed to be secret. As Remo understood the current situation, the Israeli leader was offering terms that would grant the Palestinians land in strategically debilitating areas, while the Palestinian leader was miffed because the Israelis wouldn't accept their one simple demand to lay down and stop breathing.

"Typical of white Americans," Chiun said. "You covet that which your betters have, then create an inferior copy and call it 'new.' You do not have a York, you have a New York. You cannot have a Jersey, so you make a New Jersey. And the 'new' is meant to fool people into thinking they have something that is somehow better."

Remo was not looking for news of the talks in the paper. Rather, he was scouring the personal ads, looking for anything that would seem like a possible communication between would-be terrorists. Smitty was pretty sure of himself that there was going to be a strike, and he even had an inkling of the group behind it. The trick was finding out when. At least they knew the talks were being held at the Grand Merlot, and it only took an obscene amount of money to get Remo registered there, and then double that amount to get the penthouse floor ("As befitting of a Master of Sinanju," Chiun declared). The tip to the bellhop alone would probably buy him dinner for a week, but by the time he had lugged all of Chiun's steamer trunks to their suite, he knew he'd been swindled.

"What wisdom is it you expect to find within the sheets of that dung-smattered pulp that passes for news?" Chiun asked. "Do you think your enemies will announce their plans where everyone might read them?"

"You never know," said Remo. "They're not always the brightest bulbs on the tree."

"Ah, then you are at least challenged by your equals."

"That's why I brought you along, Little Father," said

Remo. He had to admit Chiun was right, though. The odds of the terrorists sending some sort of coded message through the personals were very low. Besides, he had enough trouble deciphering "BBW SEEKS SAME 4 RP BDSM." Any one of these could be a message from one mooj to another, for all the sense it made. Remo folded the paper and tossed it onto the glass-topped table. The headline story was about a small tremor in Indonesia, and it reminded Remo of the events in Archway City.

"So you never told me," Remo said. "Did you get close to Cheeta Ching in Archway City?"

Chiun smiled beatifically. "Just to be within the same city as one with such grace and beauty is to be considered close," he said, then turned to Remo. "I could count the stitches on the hem of her impeccable dress."

Remo whistled, despite knowing Chiun could do that from with fifty yards. "That close, huh? That explains why you were a little wobbly when I found you."

"What wobbly!" Chiun spat. "A Master of Sinanju does not 'wobble!'" He glowered at Remo, but there was just a hint that something, indeed, was very wrong. Chiun calmed, his demeanor deflating. "You will notice it soon enough," he said quietly.

"Notice what?" Remo asked, mildly concerned. "What's going on that you're not telling me, Chiun?"

Before Chiun could reply, a kind of a roar, like a mosquito on steroids, came from the street above, as a pale green Volkswagen Beetle careened toward the plaza in front of the Grand Merlot.

"Looks like the mountain is going to come to Mohammed after all," Remo said, sprinting up the steep sandy incline from the beach to the hotel. He could see the Beetle now, pinging off of trashcans, vendor carts, and some of the slower pedestrians. Human screams mingled with the tiny car's whine, and Remo crested the incline just in time to see several men lounging about in casual dress suddenly spring to attention and draw concealed weapons on the Bug.

"Not the most subtle approach," Remo muttered. "No one ever said these bozos were smart, but I always figured them to be smarter than this."

"Perhaps they are," said Chiun, who was suddenly standing beside Remo. "Look."

Chiun extended a frail-looking arm in the opposite direction of the car's approach, where a lone figure wearing a bulky padded jacket was darting into an alley alongside the hotel's service entrance.

"He doesn't look like the caterer to me," Remo said, as he crossed toward the man, taking quick strides. He saw the now no-longer-undercover guards firing bullets into the front of the VW. "The motor is in the back, you morons," he called out helpfully, before slipping into the same alley his target had taken. He kicked off the wall and propelled himself to the top of a dumpster, silent as cotton falling on snow. He leaped toward the wall again, and his legs recoiled to push him toward the other side of the narrow alley, where he repeated the procedure at the opposing wall. In three strides, Remo was running silently down the alley, twenty feet in the air. When he was a few feet past the suspicious looking character in the padded jacket, he dropped to the ground in front of him.

"The hotel prefers all guests check in through the main lobby, sir," Remo said, and then shrugged. "It's policy."

The man froze for a moment, panicked. This was not supposed to happen. Men did not just drop from the sky. He looked briefly upward to see if any more American angels were about to descend before reaching into his jacket and pulling a pistol.

"You will not stop me," he said in a thick accent. The gun trembled in his hand as he aimed it at Remo. "Allah has blessed me to be his destroyer!"

Remo arched an eyebrow. "He's doing that now? I'm going to have to have a chat with him someday."

Before the gunman could pull the trigger, the disassembled gun was tinkling to the pavement in a shower of metal fragments. "You really didn't think you were going to do much damage with that little pea-shooter, did you?"

Panic-stricken, the man opened wide his bulky jacket, revealing a device like Remo had never seen before, but the purpose of which he could easily deduce. It was all yellow plastic and wires, and belted around his waist. He produced a push-button remote in his other hand, holding it up. "I'll set it off. I swear it!" he said, as sweat beaded up on his forehead.

Remo sighed and shook his head. As easily as he had

taken the gun, the remote was suddenly in Remo's grasp, leaving the would-be bomber open-mouthed and empty-handed.

"Now, why don't we have a little talk about the nice people you work for?"

"I live to serve Allah!" he declared with a stutter.

"I already guessed that, but I don't really need to go that far up the food chain," Remo said. "How about you just tell me the name of the guy you get your orders from?" Getting no immediate answer, Remo pressed one finger into the hollow of the man's left shoulder. "Any time now, if you don't mind. I've got a beach chair and an expense account, and I'd like to get back to using both of them."

The man tried to tell Remo off—that the army of ya Homaar would never submit to the infidels of the Great Satan, that the day was coming with American pigs would lie smoldering in the streets while his people took their rightful place ruling the world. He tried to say all this, but the only sound coming from his lips was one of girlish pain. "Aieeeeeee!" he cried, crumpling to his knees.

Remo removed the pressure. "Get the point," he said. "Now, let's try this again. Who..." A high pitched whining sound emanating from the man's chest interrupted him.

"What? What are you doing?" asked the man, hearing nothing. Remo leaned in close, his ear turned toward the device still strapped around the terrified ya Homaar soldier.

The pitch intensified at a consistent rate. Remo looked at the remote. No, he hadn't accidentally pressed any triggers.

The remote wasn't making any indication that it had been activated. This was something else.

"I think it's time to feed the seagulls," Remo said, picking the man up by his belt loops and running him down the alley, toward the beach.

"Wait! Allah save me!" the man wailed. Remo exited the alley, darting around the crumpled wreck of the VW Beetle where it rested against a telephone pole, surrounded by men in baggy shorts and paisley shirts holding weapons drawn. The would-be bomber then had a brainstorm—the bomb around him must be about to go off! "Take it off me! Take it off!" he screamed, scratching at the device uselessly. But it had been locked on to him when he left the compound, so that even if he wanted to take it off, he could not.

"Sorry, Moe," Remo said as he reached the edge of the incline that led down to the sand and surf. "You knew what you signed up for when you got this gig." He spun once, twice, three times, holding the man by his belt loops before releasing him in a high arc out into the open air. The man screamed and flapped his arms desperately to avoid hitting the ground. He failed, and his body impacted the sand with a crunch at just the same time that his body became the core of an explosion so devastating that it shattered some of the windows of the Grand Merlot, knocking some of the armed guards and several photo-snapping bystanders to the ground.

Remo gave a low whistle, surprised at the magnitude of the blast. "That was no dynamite belt," he said to himself, as chunks of terrorist rained down on to the beach and street.

Had he known how large the explosion would be, he'd have hurled the exploding trash bag further out into the ocean.

The explosion sent a small flock of seagulls scattering for their lives, only to return moments later for the newfound feast that now littered the beach.

CHAPTER FIVE

"THAT WAS IMPRESSIVE."

Remo turned toward the voice. The explosion hadn't so much as moved him, but the bombshell before him now rocked him all the way down to his heels. She wore an ankle length white skirt patterned with a grey pencil mural of a landscape. Upstairs, she had on a sleeveless white top that hugged the concave shape of her waistline and a neckline that scooped down to reveal one shoulder. Her dark hair was braided and lay across her covered shoulder.

"Well, what can I say?" Remo shrugged. "Some days, you just can't get rid of a bomb."

She smiled. "You didn't seem to have any trouble." She opened her purse and produced a business card. "Avital Fuchs," she announced, extending the card to Remo.

"You what?"

She had the decency to blush but was not deterred. "I'm a reporter with the *Israel Times*," she continued.

"Do you know Cheeta Ching?" The sing-song cadence carried a hopeful tone, as Chiun appeared beside Remo, seemingly from nowhere, taking the woman aback.

"Chiun, where the hell did you go?"

Chiun waved an arm at the commotion on the street above, as police cars had begun to arrive and news stations started to set up their cameras. "Here. There. I get around. The beach is quite serene. And I had lottery tickets to return for money."

"What did you do with the losers?"

Chiun huffed. "The store clerk would not take them back, even though I assured him they were untouched and still in quite sellable condition." He smiled. "In the end, I found someone who wished to feel the thrill of losing their money, and enabled them to find this beatific bliss."

"You sold them tickets that you knew were losers."

"I did not wish to burden them with knowledge that might rob them of their bliss," Chiun replied.

Avital looked up nervously at the gathering crowd. "Perhaps we could go talk someplace a bit more private?" she urged.

"Fine with me," Remo said. "I think Michelin's on their way to collect some of their stars from this place."

"But do you know Cheeta Ching?" Chiun insisted.

"She's...in New York," Avital confessed. "I don't really travel in the same circles as she does."

"Bah," Chiun waved dismissively, having no further use for this reporter. He walked ahead of them down the beach, and Avital arched one eyebrow with curiosity at how the strange little man in the bright yellow kimono managed to leave no footprints in the sand.

She turned her attention back to Remo. "So, what were your impressions of Mahboob?"

He shrugged his shoulders. "Upright. Firm. Better than average."

"Excuse me?"

"No, better than average is good. I figure a 38C, like the other one. I mean, I've seen bigger, but bigger isn't always better."

She smacked his shoulder playfully and laughed musically. "No, you idiot. I mean our human bomb back there. Mahboob Wais Vermani. He was with the ya Homaar."

"Seriously, his name was Mahboob? I would have blown myself up a long time ago."

She smirked. "And what do I call *you*, Mister...?"

Remo had known this lady less than three minutes, and had already gotten more information out of her than he had old Mahboob. He offered his hand. "Robespierre," Remo said. She took it, taking notice of the near lack of a defined wrist, as though the man's forearms went straight on into his thumb and little finger.

"Robespierre?" she asked, arching one perfect eyebrow.

"Remo Robespierre," he replied. "Just call me Remo. Everybody does. And you've already met Chiun."

"She does not know Cheeta Ching," Chiun called back. "Leave her be and let us be gone."

She smiled, and let go of his hand. "And what do you do, Mister...Remo? Besides do a mean hammer throw with exploding terrorists, that is?"

"Oh, I'm a reporter too," Remo said. "Fieldwork mostly. I don't get in front of the camera. I'm told I don't photograph all that well. I'm with...MSM-BS," he said. She gave him a doubtful look, so he added, "It's a local cable channel. Hardly anyone really watches it."

"Ah," she said, not completely convinced. "I'm surprised that a local American affiliate would send someone to cover...events here in Jersey."

She was being intentionally coy, so Remo decided to cut through the façade. "Oh, you mean the secret peace talks? Yeah, that stuff goes over big with our audience. They get together later that night at the corner café and debate the issues we air. Mostly, though, they just debate which weather girl looks the hottest, and which talking head should go back to doing sports."

Avital's eyes widened. "So you were aware of the proceedings? That explains why ya Homaar was here."

"How do you figure that?" he asked.

"Well, if *my* people knew about the secret talks, and *your* people knew about the secret talks, they really couldn't be that much of a secret, could they?"

Remo had to admit the lady had a point. "Once it gets past more than five people, secrets are impossible to keep," he said, recalling something someone had told him early in his career at CURE.

"Five?" she said with a mild scoff. "I'd always heard that it was two could keep a secret, if one of them were dead. I think that's an old Chinese proverb or something."

"Korean," Chiun called, before muttering, in Korean, something about misappropriation, plagiarism, and visiting a scourge upon someone's house.

"I like that," Remo said. "I think I'll steal it. If you don't mind, that is?" He stopped and looked into her brown eyes, his own steely orbs taking on an uncharacteristic charm.

She returned the gaze. "You're welcome to anything I have," she said, stepping well into his personal space. "Perhaps we could talk about things later? Over dinner, perhaps? I promise, my hotel doesn't have anyone trying to blow it up."

"That you know of," Remo added.

"Are you aware of something I'm not?" She arched an eyebrow and rested her hand so delicately on his shoulder that it was like it wasn't even there.

"Sweetheart, you'd be surprised," he replied with confidence.

"Good," she said. "I despise boring dinner conversation. Shall we say 8 o'clock?"

"Make it 7," Remo said. "I like to get to bed early."

She blushed. "Them let's make it 6," she purred. "I'm staying at La Haule Manor."

Remo whistled. "Pretty fancy digs for a reporter."

She looked back over her shoulder at Remo. "It's a national paper. Almost *everybody* reads it," she teased. Remo watched her walk away, timing the tick-tock sway of her departing derriere.

• • •

"They're called the ya Homaar," Remo spoke into the phone. He was sitting at an outdoor table at a café that specialized in something it called "Korean Fusion." Chiun, after making a cursory study of the menu, had decided to have words with the chef, which seemed like a good time for Remo to make a personal phone call to Smitty. It wasn't privacy, but with everyone's attention on the string of Korean and English profanity emanating from the kitchen, it was almost better.

"I'll look into them," Smitty said, the sour terseness of his voice somehow managing to lose none of its potency even across thousands of miles, two satellites, and some electronic disassembly and reassembly. "Can you trust this source?"

"She says she's a reporter or something," says Remo.

"'She,'" Smitty repeated. "Of course you trust her."

"Well, there's trust and then there's trust," Remo said. "If you mean do I trust that she knows what she's talking about when it comes to these yahoos, then yeah. If you mean do I trust that she's a reporter, not a chance. She's way too smart."

"And what did you tell her you were?" Smitty asked.

"A reporter."

"Maybe she'll buy that."

"I thought I sold it rather well. By the way, I'm going to need a new hotel room. My last one is covered in shattered glass. Any openings at La Haule Manor?"

There was a pause on the other end, and Remo could picture Smitty pinching his sinuses with frustration. "Is it completely necessary?"

"Well, I don't care, but Chiun saw the brochures and said something about surroundings befitting the Master of Sinanju, yada-yada. He's right here, if you'd like to speak to him about it."

Remo heard the sound of keys tapping. "You're on the top floor."

"Which room?"

"All of them," Smitty asked. "Try not to burn the place down."

"Pleasure doing business with you, Smitty." He winced only a little at the sound of the phone being slammed down on the American end of the communication, and thought about how elated Chiun would be at the upgrade.

A saucepan flew out into the street and embedded itself handle-first into a light post, which pretty much guaranteed the chef wasn't the pitcher. "Guess I'd better go cancel this season of Hell's Café," he said, standing up and heading into the rapidly-evacuating restaurant.

CHAPTER SIX

REVEREND BILLY WALKER HAD NOT BEEN GIVEN the title "America's Pastor." He had earned it. He had always followed the scriptures assiduously, since even before he attended Bible College. He had tended his flock above all his own matters. He had even foregone forging a family of his own to grow the family of God.

Ultimately, though, he owed his greatest stroke of fortune to a devil.

Walker's office was never what one could call ostentatious, although it could have been and nobody would have faulted him for it. Walker's books were always open, his accounting activities blatantly transparent—so consistently transparent for so many years that now auditors barely glanced at them. His desk was a dark mahogany—real furniture, not typical office supply store variety—and the bookshelves lining two walls from floor to ceiling were filled with a variety of texts ranging from theology to geological surveys to military technical manuals. Walker's interests ranged a wide gamut.

Almost none of it meant anything to Walker. They were

merely worldly possessions, and his treasures were stored up elsewhere. Still, the Reverend Billy Walker was packing. The box was small, little more than a shoebox. His clothes had already been loaded aboard his private jet.

A private jet, Walker mused, smiling as he shook his head. He could hardly believe how far he'd come, how far God had brought him, just by being true to the Word.

It had taken him a good twenty years of preaching the gospel and saving souls to fill God's house to the rafters. And even then, his greatest pain had come from seeing believers fall away. He could add ninety-nine converts, but if he lost one he would sit up at nights agonizing in prayer for that one lost soul.

He remembered the night when the idea first came to him. He had been beseeching God for hours when he had turned on the nightly news in time to catch the first reports of the capture, introducing him to the first of two men who would forever alter the course of his life.

"...taken at Mount of Olives General by police, after leaving three more dead bodies in his wake," the pretty blonde reporter was saying, putting on her practiced 'serious' face. "If you're just joining us, a joint task force of FBI and State Police have taken into custody a man fitting the description of the wanted serial killer social media has dubbed 'The Cradle Robber.' Our cameras were on the scene to capture the end of the manhunt."

The frame cut to one of several officers manhandling a struggling young man—clean-shaven but wild-eyed, dressed in hospital scrubs. "I'm saving them!" he screamed. "They come here, and we just corrupt their innocent souls!" An officer pushed down on the man's head to get him into the back of the waiting squad car. "I'm saving their souls!" he shrieked one last time before the door was slammed shut.

"That was the scene at Mount of Olives General," the blonde reporter's voice narrated, "after a nurse reported an unfamiliar person administering immunizations in the obstetrics unit, which turned out to be syringes of air. Three babies died of embolisms, bringing the killer's death toll to twenty-three."

Walker had turned off the television in disgust, praying for the serenity and peace of the bereaved parents. But the so-called Cradle Robber had awakened something in him—an idea he could understand, even though that understanding disgusted him at first.

It would be a few years later when divine providence would open another door for the Reverend, when he sat down at that same mahogany desk, took a sip of his black morning coffee, and opened up his newspaper. Staring up from the front page of *The Clarion* was his own face.

He wasn't all that surprised. It was in vogue at the time to dig up dirt on those who had made a life of doing the Lord's work. Hypocrisy was taking down nationally recognized evangelical figures left and right, as investigative inquiries turned up everything from drugs to promiscuity to prostitution.

The story from *The Clarion* was one of embezzling,

claiming that Walker's local megachurch was as rife with corruption as all the nationally famous ones that were falling from grace.

It was an easy story to believe, because pastors were assumed to live in poverty. A photo of Walker's nice house, a rundown of the costs of his suits and his car—it was all people would need to believe that the pastor was helping himself to funds he should not. The reporter, one Jacob Riser, was making a bold statement—one he must have assumed he would not have to support beyond the superficial. After all, a good Christian was supposed to turn the other cheek.

Walker turned the other cheek in the direction of his phone, which he used to dial his attorney. By the end of the day, *The Clarion* had been served with a defamation lawsuit. Twenty-two hours and an editorial board meeting later, the newspaper decided it would not change its position, and would let Walker's challenge be determined by a jury—a trial *The Clarion* planned to cover extensively, with early and updated editions every day. What they had not counted on was just how wrong they were. By the end of the suit, nobody trusted *The Clarion* to wrap fish. Their competition took to referring to their stories as "Jell-o urinalism," a term which meant nothing and yet communicated everything.

What was also unexpected was America's response to the whole thing. America had searched in desperation for an honest man, and had found one in the Reverend Billy Walker. When Walker, much to the chagrin of his attorneys, asked the jury to lower the award fee to just his legal costs and a printed retraction, America fell completely in love with the humble preacher. Walker's ministry was suddenly coast-to-coast, and the money came flooding in from all corners. Suddenly, Billy Walker was an insanely wealthy man, who reinvested his wealth in America, creating jobs across the country, initially by opening consignment clothing and household goods stores to serve as job training for the homeless and undereducated, before later moving into investments to make America energy independent. And yet, all the wealth in the world could not erase the guilt and sorrow he felt when people fell away from the faith. If anything, it magnified the feeling, because his flock had grown from thousands to millions.

And then he met the girls.

Billy Walker liked to work at the personal level, something he found harder to do as his congregation began to number in the thousands. So when he travelled from city to city, he made it a practice to slip out without an entourage and minister where he could to the lost, the homeless, and the helpless. And on one such night, in Sacramento, he came across the sisters. Having lost their father, they found themselves without a means of support, and were making a living prostituting themselves out as a duo. They were bedraggled, desperate, and full of worldly notions. When they came up to him, they asked him if he wanted a 'job.' He smiled, and told them that he already had one. This made them giggle, which he found infectious. He then asked about their needs, which were simple: money.

Often when he would be asked for money, he would find himself quoting Peter. *"Silver and gold, have I none"*. Only that wasn't true any longer. He had silver and gold in plenty.

He offered to buy them dinner. They accepted the offer, then seemed to be taken aback that he drove them to a restaurant, and a nice one at that. When the waiter turned up his nose at their attire, Billy pretended not to notice while also assertively assuring that they were treated with respect.

They ate. They talked. And when the girls realized their clever little innuendos and subtle overtures didn't faze him, they talked about other things. And Billy Walker learned these girls had a depth of intelligence and experience uncommon among the homeless.

In the end, the girls who had offered him a job were offered jobs themselves, which they accepted.

Later that next week, he saved their souls during a tent revival meeting in Los Angeles, and they had been part of his organization ever since.

And then one night, as he began to lament once more in his office, they overheard his sobs. He shared his dreadful dream with them, and they shared their knowledge. What wonderfully smart girls they turned out to be! It was then Walker knew that the crossing of their paths was fate. Together, the three of them spread Walker's ideals to all the right people. Walker invested heavily into worldwide oil exploration and then, more recently, sold off those operations to invest in mining and urban gentrification projects. The public followed his every move, and applauded his providing jobs with each project.

He was well down the path now, and victory was all but assured. When he thought about *The Clarion* these days, and the disgraced reporter who set the ball rolling, he understood how Joseph felt confronting his brothers after spending years of slavery in Egypt. *"Ye thought evil against me, but God meant it unto good,"* he would mutter to himself with a smile.

And now he was packing. A knock at the door made Walker look up from his reveries, greeted by the curvaceous bodies of the two girls whose conservative attire did little to hide the earthly pleasures of their flesh. He'd long ago fallen in love with them both, despite the chasm of years between his age and theirs. But being a godly man who would never fornicate outside the bonds of marriage, he remained chaste. However, he often entertained the notion that perhaps, just perhaps, those gentlemen in Utah were onto something righteous and holy after all. After all, didn't Jacob take two wives to himself and birth a nation through them?

"It's time," said the first girl.

"The plane's all warmed up, and so are we," purred the second.

The Reverend Walker could not suppress a smile when he looked up to see his beautiful helpers silhouetted in the doorway of his office. He blushed at their forwardness, a quality he at first tried to tame but later learned to just accept. They were precious to him, young and full of life and so ready and eager for…

He shook the thought out of his head. "I'll be right there, sweethearts," he said. "Just making sure I'm not leaving behind anything important."

"We'll be waiting on board," the first girl said with a giggle. They turned away, slowly, their behinds swaying in synchronized rhythm like upside-down hearts on two pendulums. He sighed. They were as lovely going as they were coming, he thought, then mentally chided himself for the lustful thoughts.

Walker took one last glance around the room. Then, finding nothing else he absolutely needed, he put the lid on the small box of his necessities, among which were his worn-out well-read copy of the King James Bible and a seldom-used .38 snub-nosed revolver. Then he tucked the box under his arm and thought about tomorrow, wondering, as he often did, whether it was a day that would actually happen—whether this day would be the day that began eternity for everyone. He could only hope, but he was more certain than ever of two things: God would return, and he would be alive to see it.

As he shut the door, he happily murmured a tuneful congregational hymn under his breath. *"As I'm bid-ding, this world, good-bye."*

CHAPTER SEVEN

"ROBESPIERRE?"

"He says he's a reporter." Avital Avraham brushed the back of her impeccable nails against her peach pashmina scarf. "But I don't believe him. He's not smart enough."

"He is American." The man sitting across the table from her offered this as though it were an explanation for everything.

She shrugged. "True," she said. "But my instincts say he is CIA, or perhaps DHS."

"How much did he know about the ya Homaar?"

Ephraim Ben-David had been a Mossad gathering officer for over ten years now. Management had made his midsection softer, but his mind was still as sharp as when he was a field agent. He took out a handkerchief and wiped his brow, then adjusted his yarmulke, which threatened to slide off the back of his head. He hated meeting in darkened back rooms to coordinate information. It felt like something out of a bad spy movie—an American spy movie—but the budget was small, and so his cover was to live in a tiny apartment above the delicatessen that he ran as a cover. The salty smell of salami wafted up from the store below. His yarmulke was tufted with hair in an effort to hide his orthodoxy from customers.

"He pretended not to know anything," she said, crossing her legs in a relaxed fashion that left Ephraim feeling anything but relaxed. "But he knew about the negotiations, so he's definitely a player at some level."

"What about the Asian you said was with him?" Ephraim asked. He popped an antacid to quell the rising fire in his esophagus. "Could he be an American operative for the MSS?"

Avital's eyes twinkled with amusement, which somehow made her appear all the more dangerous. "I don't think so, but if the Institute has taught me anything it's that anything is possible." She smiled, and her perfect teeth reflected the light with a sparkle. "At any rate, I have a date with him for…dinner. So by the next day I'll know everything about him."

Ephraim held up both hands. "I don't need to know the details," he said, stopping Avital from *tachless*, from getting to the point. He longed for a more civilized time when information extraction relied on civilized means, like rubber hoses, alligator clips, and car batteries. He found the *katsa*'s softer methods to be unseemly; he despised the use of a "honey trap." But he couldn't deny she got more than her expected share of human intelligence, HUMINT, from her assignments. There used to be hushed talk that Avital Avraham could have a recruit begging to spill information and spill their seed in the same breath. There used to be hushed talk—until Avital herself walked in on one of the conversations, and openly began telling tales of conquest with a level of detail that none of the whisperers would have dared to imagine. After that, the conversations didn't have to be so hushed.

Avital was acutely aware of her handler's discomfort, which only made her want to go into more detail. She imagined the somewhat-handsome American drooling on the bed, his overstimulated limbic system draining all the mental dampers around the secrets he kept. She flushed hotly at the thought, and crossed her legs in the other direction, clenching her thighs a bit more tightly.

"When we assigned you to this *yarid*," Ephraim chided, "it was to find out how these worthless indigents of ya Homaar suddenly came into such devastating weapons. For years, they were only a threat to the goats that wander their mountains. Now, four bombings within Israel—one in Jerusalem! One that nearly devastated our Knesset."

She sighed. "I am aware, sir," she said. "I'll try to rein in my...zeal. If we have anything in our favor, it is that they still remain somewhat inept despite their inexplicable weapons gains."

It was true. Each bombing had been within moments and blocks of being major catastrophes. The first bombing had taken killed a roadside work crew that had temporarily blocked the road to a middle school. The second one had derailed a cargo train at a crossing only a few dozen yards from an outdoor marketplace. The last bombing had been the worst, killing over a dozen drivers who were stuck in traffic—including the bomber—due to security details around the session of the Knesset. Either these radical jihadists didn't know they were closer to a higher value target, or they had accidentally bumped their detonators. Even today their bad luck was running true to form, with the intervention of the American, Remo.

"Just find out what you can as quickly as possible," Tsalmon sighed. "We don't have time to turn a recruit. Just get the information. And remember, always: when you are with *your* friend, make sure he is not with *his*."

"Of course, sir," Avital replied. Every first year Institute recruit had the Mossad adage for handling assets. You had to be sure you were not dealing with a dangle, with someone set to trap you. And you damn sure had to be certain you didn't develop any real relationships.

Avital was about to ask if they were through, when the room shuddered. She grasped the edge of the table as though it would steady the world, as Tsalmon pushed his chair back and dove under the table for cover, giving him an unwanted but unavoidable view directly up Avital's skirt. "Bomb!" he yelled, as books and pens quivered on their shelves before falling to the floor.

Avital, still gripping the edge of the table, remained otherwise cool and observant. "I don't think so," she said, as the trembling subsided. "I think that was actually an earthquake."

"In the Channel Islands?" Tsalmon looked up at her from under the table. *Look at her eyes, look at her eyes, look at her eyes*, he repeated in his mind, from his vantage point that was parallel to her knees. "There hasn't been a noticeable earthquake here for almost a century!"

The tremor subsided, and aside from a decorative piece of pottery, the contents of Tsalmon's quarters were unharmed. Outside, a car alarm blared annoyingly.

Tsalmon started to crawl forward from under the desk, paused, then scooted backward on his hands and knees until he had reversed out from beneath the table.

Avital stood and walked, heel-toe, heel-toe to the window and pulled back the curtain. Other than a cracked plate glass window in a clothing store across the street and a hanging streetlight that had fallen on a parked car (the same car with the annoying alarm), there was little evidence that a natural disaster had just occurred.

"Well, I think we can reset the clock timing that particular event," she said coolly.

• • •

Across town, Remo was directing traffic.

"Third room from the end," he said. "On the left. The others are already filled to the gills."

The parade of movers and hand-trucks grunted and squeaked, carrying a seemingly never-ending stream of steamer trunks to the top floor of the La Haule Manor.

At the far end of the hallway stood Chiun, his arms crossed imperiously, hands tucked into the sleeves of a silk kimono so black it vigorously sucked in all the light around it. His eyes appeared almost closed, but each mover was keenly aware that he was monitoring them.

"Easy on that corner, Joe," said the older man who was supervising the transition. "That's fine teak on that one." He gave the chest a loving stroke, earning a barely perceptible raised eyebrow from Chiun, a silent approval given to someone who appreciated fine art. "Take a wide swing so you don't..."

He was cut off as the floor began to undulate. Joe lost his grip on the hand-truck, the steamer trunk slipping off its ledge and sliding toward the doorjamb. Joe reached for it, seeing it slip away as if in slow motion. Suddenly, an arm reached over his shoulder, a forearm that seemed to go directly into a very fast hand without bothering to taper into a wrist. The hand caught the far edge of the trunk, pulling it back from the wall with inches to spare.

"Earthquake!" Remo yelled. "Everyone, find a doorway and stand in it!"

Slightly more than a dozen workers stumbled from their chores into the doorways lining the upper floor of La Haule Manor. Remo surveyed the hallway, making sure everyone was safe, that nobody was hurt, as the chandeliers began to swing faster and harder. He was surrounded by chaos, but that was just another Thursday. And then Remo saw something that made his blood run cold.

He saw Chiun.

And Chiun was on the ground.

"I think he's going to be okay, son. Just took a little spill." The near-retirement supervisor—Leonard, according to the nametag on his coveralls—placed a hand on Remo's shoulder, meant to comfort him. Chiun was seated now, and Remo was kneeling on the floor beside him.

Cold eyes, set deep beneath a furrowed brow, cut to the hand on his shoulder. Then they closed once, and reopened, much softened. "Thanks," Remo said, rising to his feet. "Tell you what, Stanley. All the trunks, they're off the trucks right?"

"Just got about eighteen more down in the lobby, but yeah," Stanley said.

"I'll get them," Remo said. He pulled out his wallet and peeled out twenty 100 Euro notes. "Why don't you guys knock off for a bit? Go get some beers, calm some nerves. It's been a heck of a day for all of us."

"Mister, the bill's only a thousand."

"Call it hazard pay," Remo said warmly, handing the money over. He didn't add that they were going to get it anyway, as moving trunks for the Master of Sinanju was about as hazardous a job as any man might undertake.

Leonard laughed nervously. "Well, sir, if you say so." He handed over Remo's copy of the invoice. "You need anything moved again, you know who to call."

"You bet, Leonard."

He waited until the men had packed all the hand-trucks into the service elevators. As soon as the doors closed, he wheeled back to Chiun.

"Little Father." He knelt again beside the frail old figure. Remo realized for the first time Chiun actually did appear old and frail to him, and that gave him a feeling he had not felt in a long time: fear. "What happened?"

Chiun looked up at Remo, his lips pursed in indignation. "An earthquake happened," he said. "Things move in earthquakes. Entire buildings fall down in them. Certainly a person can expect to stumble."

"Chiun, I've seen you run a sprint in an earthquake before," Remo said. "You didn't even so much as kick a pebble, let alone fall down. So don't give me that. What's really going on?"

Chiun jutted out his chin defiantly, but Remo didn't relent.

"What's wrong, Little Father?" he asked again. "Are you...Are you dying?"

Chiun looked down and away. His shoulders began to shake up and down, and it was moments before Remo realized the old master was laughing, albeit sadly.

"Yes," Chiun said, finally. "Yes, I am dying. I am dying, you are dying, we are all dying."

"I know that," Remo said.

"Yes," Chiun said. "But now we are all dying much faster." He sat, and Remo's senses went on full alert. Nothing required Chiun to sit.

"The earth cries out in pain," Chiun finally said. "I know you can feel it."

Remo had been feeling something the past few days akin to car sickness. He had been ignoring it, writing it off to some virus whose ass his system was no doubt kicking. "What am I feeling, Little Father?" he asked.

Chiun folded his arms. "Sinanju is breathing," he began, going back to the primal lessons he had given Remo on their very first day of training. "You breathe to fullness. You center yourself. This is the core of the sun source."

Remo stood silent, stock still as Chiun paused.

"But what is centered, when there is nothing to center against?" Chiun finally stated. "The earth is crying out, like a new mother in labor." He looked up at Remo, and his eyes, which were normally vellum slits of condescending wisdom, were now open fully, and brimming with sadness.

"A great death is being born."

CHAPTER EIGHT

HAROLD W. SMITH WAS A MAN who kept up on current events. It was the very definition of his work. If he was the sort of man who had friends, he could have been a brilliant and depressing conversationalist. Everybody wants to know the latest news. Unfortunately, far fewer people want to know one more way the country may be headed for disaster.

Even so, ya Homaar was something barely on his radar, and with good reason. Until very recently, the would-be terror group never existed. The first mention of them Smith found was in some encrypted CIA messages the CURE computer had intercepted and decoded, regarding a faction that had split off from Daesh over the fundamentals of whether martyrs of jihad were going to get seventy-two virgins in heaven, or seventy and two virgins, with ya Homaar proposing the latter meant they would receive two virgins and seventy of some other unknown treasure. There were a few beheadings over the dogmatic schism, and when it was over those who survived formed ya Homaar and took to hiding in the caves of Afghanistan. They never did make clear what the other seventy might mean, but they had ideas that it must be something better than virgins.

Smith had the CURE systems run a full cross-reference on all known ya Homaar survivors and their whereabouts. He furrowed his brow in frustration that the system persisted in dragging in stories about global tremors, obscuring any real national threats, but he hadn't yet had the opportunity to bring the matter to the programmers. He grabbed the floating object of earthquake stories and dragged it over to the recycle bin. This forced the latest ya Homaar references into the foreground, and he searched through them for potential threats. Finding nothing, he implemented a search across all the other systems that made up the true depth of CURE's reach, and then moved on to systems used by hackers and trolls like Incognito and Forchun. Smith found the users there puerile and attention-hungry, but their access to information through social media was unparalleled, so long as it was filtered by something as uninterested in gossip as the CURE search engine — or Smith himself.

Smith found an airline passenger manifest a few months back that included one Abdel Kassab, formerly a student at the University of Cairo who had abandoned the pursuit of his doctorate in neuroscience for a career in making online videos shouting "Death to America" as frequently as possible. The itinerary placed him in Los Angeles. By the time Smith had read that far, the system was already employing facial recognition to every captured image from surveillance cameras all around the city, following him to the taxi stand outside LAX, to a traffic light in Burbank where his cab driver ran through a red light, and ultimately to the foyer of the Billy Walker Evangelistic Outreach Watchtower.

Smith wondered what would bring an insurgent like Abdel to the home of what he would consider the greatest infidel America could produce. Smith knew the building hadn't suffered an attack, but that didn't mean that Kassab hadn't left something behind that was yet to be felt. He called up all the footage from the building, and watched as Abdel paced nervously in the foyer before going directly to the information desk. A few minutes later, he was allowed passage through the turnstile where he took an elevator to the top floor.

Several minutes later, Kassab returned to the foyer, looking dazed with bliss. He looked up, laughed, and then skipped to the exit with the exuberance of a child. Smith followed him back into another cab, through two more red-light cameras, and back to LAX where he purchased a one-way ticket to Herat. Shortly after that, ya Homaar began to bubble up in the headlines of terrorist attacks—somewhat bungled ones, though still resulting in the loss of lives. The attacks were focused in the Middle East, but were also occurring at random around the world.

Smith didn't like the implications. The notion that someone within Walker's organization was funneling money to a terrorist organization was incomprehensible. Unless, Smith thought, someone had intentionally infiltrated the work of "America's Pastor" with the intention of using the charitable organization's vast wealth for other purposes.

Smith added the Evangelistic Outreach Watchtower to the keywords of the computer's regular list of triggers. Almost immediately the system brought up a page 12 story from the *Los Angeles Times* about a mugging-turned-murder. A man, Jacob Riser, had been found in an alleyway, his wallet and life both stolen from him. Crime scene photographs began to sprout up next to the article, showing Riser's lifeless body, face down on the pavement, his left hand extended outward above his body. Optical character recognition subroutines boxed any letters in the image and represented them in plain text. Graffiti on the wall was sorted to the bottom of the extracted words as irrelevant or meaningless. Appearing at the top of each list for each picture, however, was a numerical representation: 1:49. Smith peered at the photo and saw it was smeared on the lower corner of the garbage dumpster near Riser. It seemed obvious the numbers were written by the dying man in his own blood, but there was nothing in the police reports about it. Smith frowned. It was no surprise. The last thing any beat cop wants is a Raymond Chandler mystery interfering with his pursuit of a pension.

But what was the connection to Walker? What algorithm caused the system to highlight this event? Smith called up the digitized evidence locker to see what else might be important. Aside from the discarded wallet, the police had collected: one cellular phone (broken from impact), one keychain (with three keys), one page of itinerary, and two rabbit's foot charms.

The LAPD had thoughtfully taken digital images of all the items, saving Smith the need to have someone examine the physical evidence. Smith looked at the aforementioned itinerary sheet, which was little more than a list of cities and timestamps, none of which matched up to any events on his radar. He dragged a copy of the image over to his desktop for later analysis, and moved on to the cellular phone.

Within moments, Smith had pulled up a list of Riser's calls, including one made only minutes before his demise to a Chicago number. The police had no doubt called the number, but Smith was just as sure that they had asked all the wrong questions. He punched in a sequence of numbers, then added the last number from Riser's history. The phone on the other end would display an incoming call from *Pinnacle News*, which could be verified if the person felt the need to do so. Most didn't.

The phone rang twice.

"Yeah?" the voice sounded from the other end.

"Mr. Schultz, please," Smith said.

"Take me off your list," Schultz said, right before the line went dead. Smith redialed. He dialed again. The phone continued going to voice mail.

A few keystrokes, and Smith found another number and dialed it.

After one ring, Smith got a response, "Yeah?" Apparently Schultz didn't have a *Hello* in him.

"Mr. Schultz, my name is Harold Smith, and…"

"Boy, you got some nerve, calling me up at my place of business. You know my cell phone is on the Do Not Call list! I should have you reported."

Smith let him rant, then interrupted. "Mr. Schultz, I'm not calling to sell you anything. I'm calling about Jacob Riser."

That earned Smith a pause from Schultz. "Yeah, I know. I heard," Schultz finally said. "I already talked to the cops, so I know you're not a cop. What's your angle?"

Smith cleared his throat. This Schultz was not one for small talk. Smith's admiration for him was instant, so he cut to the chase. "Billy Walker."

"Ah, Christ," Schultz moaned. "Even in death, Riser's killing me."

So there was a connection after all, Smith mused. "Can you help me out?" Smith asked. "What was the story between those two?"

Schultz sighed. "Look, if you're trying to put together a piece on Walker based on Jake's death, let me give you some free advice. Don't do it. You can thank me when you retire with your 401k intact."

"I'm going to need more information than that," Smith pressed. "Did they have a history?"

"History!" Schultz barked a laugh. "Yeah, you could call it that. You really don't know, do you?" He exhaled, preparing to launch into a story he did not like telling. "Fine, but do me a favor. Leave me out of it, okay?"

Smith averred that Schultz's name wouldn't be published

in any story he wrote. Which, since he didn't plan on writing anything, and didn't have the imagination for such a thing in the first place, was the truth.

"All right," Schultz said. "This was years ago, see? You couldn't turn on the tube without seeing some story about one famous religious guy or another getting outed with a prostitute or scamming his followers. It was the hot topic. You get one of those stories, you got instant audience, you know?"

Smith made a grunt of acknowledgment as if he remembered the time well and understood exactly what Schultz meant.

"So Jake, he's just this cub reporter, right? And he's eager. He's a decent writer, and he's had a couple of breaks on the Chicago crime beat, so people are starting to notice him. I'd taken him under my wing, all right? Mentored him a little. Don't write that down, though."

"No, of course not," Smith said.

"So anyway, Jake's not blind," Schultz continued. "He's hungry, and he sees which way the wind is blowing. So he says he's looking into Walker. Back then, Walker wasn't famous. Not nationally. He was something of a local celebrity, though. Had a megachurch just down in Lockport. Did a weekly show every Sunday morning. And Jake, he figures maybe he can find something, get a good local story."

Smith couldn't see where this was going. Was Riser killed out of some kind of revenge for exposing something about Walker so long ago? "What did he find?" he asked.

"Bupkus!" Schultz said. "But we didn't know that. He came in with some bullshit story about embezzlement and scamming—the usual spiel that matched so many other guys, you know? I guess that's why it was so believable." He paused. "I vouched for that son of a bitch," he added bitterly. "So *The Clarion* ran the story. Walker sued. Not that I blame him for that. The boys, they were so invested now in Jake's story being on the up and up, they wouldn't settle out of court and retract. They forced it into court. And let me tell you, *that* got an audience!"

Schultz was on a roll now, and didn't need any prompting from Smith. "In the end, the jury awarded him a cool million. And you know what he did? He dropped it to court costs. All he wanted was for the paper to print a retraction. And he *still* got rich. You know why? Because America saw something they thought didn't exist—an honest man. That little Sunday morning show of his went national. Money came pouring in like water, and every penny of it went exactly where Walker told everyone it did. He's got the big fancy glass tower on the west coast now, a global operation. And he still pulls down pretty much the same salary he always has."

"I don't understand," Smith said. "This was years ago. Was Jacob Riser still pursuing Walker on the night he died?"

"He just couldn't let it go," Schultz said. "He'd lost his job, his credibility. Best he could do was write tabloid crap, and even that he had to do with a pseudonym. But he always kept one eye on Walker, always waited for the guy to trip up so he could have his vindication. Poor son of a bitch. So that night, he calls me up, says he's finally got something, something big."

"Did he say what it was?" Smith asked.

"I didn't give him a chance," Schultz said. "Fool me once, you know? I told him to take a hike. Damn. That must have been just a few minutes before he got mugged in that alley. Poor son of a bitch," he repeated.

"I see," Smith said. "Thank you, Mr. Schultz. You've been very helpful."

"Who, me?" Schultz said. "I didn't say a thing. I never even heard from you."

"I understand," Smith said. "Thank you anyway." But Schultz had already disconnected.

Smith planted his elbows on his desk, propped up his chin and thought. If this Riser fellow was doggedly checking up on Walker's ministries, he might have stumbled across whoever it was in the organization who had met with ya Homaar. If so, it was quite probable Riser's death wasn't a mugging after all, and far from random.

CHAPTER NINE

IF YOU READ THE BROCHURES, THERE WASN'T a single square inch of the Channel Islands that wasn't perfect. And that was true, depending on the intent of the reader. If you were looking for beautiful shoreline and ocean breezes, then there were plenty of square inches that were perfect for you. But if you were looking for a place to operate without much in the way of surveillance, well, there were square inches that were perfect for that as well.

It was toward one of those cramped, dingy square inches that Abdel Kassab was running full tilt, clutching his *kufiya* to his head with one hand as his baggy trousers and knee-length dress flapped in the breeze created by his sprint through the alley. He risked getting shot as he burst through the rear wooden door without giving the agreed upon knock.

"Mahboob is dead," he declared, breathless. Three rifles were quickly placed back on the tables, as their startled bearers recognized Abdel moments before they would have perforated him.

The fourth man in the room looked up from his paper. "Of course Mahboob is dead, Abdel," he said coolly. "His spirit now resides in the bosom of Allah, may his name be praised from the setting of the sun to the rising of the same. He is enjoying the ministrations of his promised virgins, as befits a martyr." No one tried to create the mental picture of being ministered to by virgins while sitting on the lap of God.

"No, Javid," Abdel panted. "He failed. The Zionists still live. Only Mahboob is dead."

Javid sat up straight at full attention. "Explain," he demanded.

Abdel explained how he had observed from afar how their carefully orchestrated plan unfolded: how the diversionary vehicle driven by the blessed martyrs drew the attention of the guards, and how Mahboob so very stealthily entered the alley leading behind the Grand Merlot Valeton hotel to complete his mission of jihad. But then the plan fell apart, when the slender American man ran up from the beach and entered the alley behind Mahboob, only to exit moments later, racing with Mahboob in his arms and hurtling him over the steep embankment to the beach below, where the bomb then exploded, wasting Mahboob's life.

"The American must have detonated it with the remote," Javid said. He spat. "We will find him. We will kill him and visit the blood of jihad upon his countrymen." Javid prided himself on being an orator, and once a week insisted all his brethren participated in Speech Maestro training, a practice he had adopted years before. He stood, and walked out from behind his table, establishing his speaking area.

"Brothers of ya Homaar," he intoned. "It is with a heart heavy with the righteous anger of the ages that we bid a sorrowful farewell to our brother Mahboob. Mahboob, who has been robbed of his riches in heaven, who is now, in fact, in Hell, wailing and gnashing his teeth in agony over having failed to bring jihad to full fruition because of the actions of an American interloper."

The three other men in the room nodded in agreement, so Abdel felt he should nod as well.

Javid clenched a fist and waved it at the heavens. "This is why we fight, my brothers," he spoke. He had such conviction in his tone, nobody bothered to ask the question, "We fight because of Mahboob?" They listened with rapt attention, cheering and spurring Javid on to greater calisthenics of oratory. "This is why we must win!" he continued. "And this is why we gladly die!" This last bit was met with more cheering, and if Javid noticed that it died off a bit prematurely as the words sunk in to his audience, he didn't let it derail him.

He paced back and forth, collecting his thoughts before speaking again. "We must plan carefully to take revenge upon this American. His death must be bloody. It must be painful. But most of all, it must make headlines! Though we may not redeem our brother, Mahboob, we may certainly avenge him."

Abdel brightened. "Ah, Javid! That vengeance has been handed to us already by the grace of Allah!"

"How do you mean?" Javid asked, puzzled and perturbed

at the interruption of his great planning.

"The American spoke with a woman," said Abdel. "Immediately after Mahboob's death, he flirted with her and made arrangements for dinner at her hotel!"

"I see," Javid said, stroking his chin thoughtfully. "But how does this help our vengeance? Should we go there and capture him? Yes, this would be a good plan. We could videotape his torture and broadcast it to the Americans, to show them how weak they are against the men of ya Homaar!"

Abdel was confused. "But Javid, there is no need. The hotel, it is La Haule Manor, the very hotel where one of our brothers..." He looked about the room, his lips moving silently as he counted. "Javid, who is the martyr who is now on his way to La Haule Manor to destroy that decadent palace of capitalism while the authorities are distracted with the devastation at the Valeton?"

Javid waved a hand dismissively. "I have changed the plan," he said. "We can find a much better, more impacting target than some opulent temporary dwelling for the idle rich. We should use our power against those who would oppose us, those who should be removed from the face of the Earth, like the Americans and the Jews."

Abdel then noticed the backpack, the one holding the bomb, the bomb that was supposed to be well on its way to La Haule Manor. "But Javid," Abdel spoke urgently. "The Americans, the ones who gave us the bombs, they were very insistent that the bomb be in place for detonation at a specific time. *Very insistent!*"

Javid spat on the floor. "Is this what you have come to, Abdel, that you subjugate yourself to the childish demands and tantrums of American infidels, and women?"

Abdel looked duly chastened. "I understand, Javid," he said meekly. "I only meant that if we displease our infidel benefactors, they may not provide us with more of their arsenal in the future."

Javid smiled. "In the future, Abdel, we..."

Whatever Javid's plans for the future may have been were interrupted by the onrush of white flames that filled the room so rapidly that their sudden presence blew out both painted-over windows and splintered the door. The men inside were incinerated, then tenderized by the impact of the roof falling in on them. Of course, by that time they were quite dead, and possibly surprised to see Mahboob.

• • •

"It's not 6 o'clock yet."

Avital walked briskly up to Remo, who was standing near the police tape that cordoned off the blast area.

"What's a dinner date without a few appetizers?" Remo quipped, taking in the vision of her approach. She had only changed her skirt for a much shorter one than the one she wore earlier, but it was like he was seeing her again for the first time. He couldn't wait to see her again for the first time later that evening.

"Destruction whets your appetite?" she said, looking out over the smoking rubble. "How far did you throw this one?"

Remo raised his hands. "It wasn't me this time, I swear! I was just out taking a walk when I heard the boom."

"A likely story," Avital grinned. "And where's your friend?"

Remo's face darkened just a little at the mention of Chiun. "He was...a bit shook up by the events of the day, so I stepped out to let him get some rest." In fact, Remo had stepped out to call Smitty about his concerns with Chiun's health when he did, actually, hear the boom of the explosion and ran the several blocks toward the sound to investigate if he had missed some backup attempt by ya Homaar to take out the diplomats. But the neighborhood Remo found himself entering cleared up any concerns about that, unless diplomats had seriously lowered their standards. "What brings you here?"

She flashed a brilliant smile. "Reporter, remember? Like you, right?" Her brilliant smile collapsed into a smirk. "Explosions sell stories. Explosions are...sexy."

"Boom," Remo said softly, facing her and stepping in close. He looked deep into her brown eyes for an eternity of seconds, and could feel her getting just as lost. If it wasn't for all the rescue workers, police officers, smoke, debris, and lack of anything resembling a mattress, he was ready to mambo. Maybe she was right about him. Maybe destruction always awoke some kind of appetite in him. But then, what was her excuse for feeling the same way? *Explosions are definitely sexy*, he thought, as he noticed her nipples press against the fabric of her dress. "So what do you think happened?" he asked, forcing himself back to reality. "Ruptured gas line? Meth lab gone bad?"

Avital blinked and shook her head. "Another bomb blast," she said.

"Pretty shitty target to take out," Remo said. "If anything, they improved the neighborhood."

"It's nothing like that," she said. "At least, I don't believe it is. I had some...reliable informants. They were convinced that ya Homaar operated a cell out of this area."

"Those jackasses, again," Remo said. "Maybe they blew up their hideout on purpose to cover their tracks, but based on my encounter with McBoob, they just don't seem to know what they're doing with their bombs."

"They didn't have such capabilities until recently," Avital said, more to herself than to Remo. "All they used to do was make internet recruitment videos and beg for money."

"Either they recruited somebody smart, or they found an outside benefactor," Remo offered.

"What do you think they're getting—the money for bombs, or the bombs themselves?" Avital asked. They watched as a rescue team went through the motions of kicking through the rubble, acutely aware that there wouldn't even be recognizable body parts to salvage from the blast, let alone a survivor. "I'd love to get my hands on one of those bombs," she added.

"Have someone you want taken out that badly, do you?" Remo asked.

Avital smiled wistfully. "Well, there *was* this editor, once," she teased. "But no, I'd like to poke around inside, see what makes them tick."

"What the hell kind of journalism school did you go to that included classes in Bomb Appreciation?" Remo asked.

"My father was IDF," she said. "Yahalom," she added, as though that should explain everything. When she saw from Remo's blank expression that it did not, she continued. "Special operations, you would call it. He specialized in explosive ordnance disposal."

"And he taught his little girl all his tricks, I suppose."

Avital shrugged. "When he wasn't teaching me how to shoot the balls off an attacker at eighty yards."

"Ouch."

"I'm kidding," she said. "I read a lot. He had manuals."

"You know, most teenage girls I know go in for stories about vampires with glittery makeup, not military textbooks about which bomb wire to cut."

"I was *never* your typical teenage girl," she winked.

Remo gave her a lopsided grin. "I can imagine," he said. "So you actually understood all that stuff and remembered it?"

"You should see the things I learned from the Kama Sutra."

"Is it 6 o'clock yet?"

"Close enough."

"Give me five minutes, I need to make a quick phone call."

"So do I," she said. She slipped him a card. "My spare room key," she said. "Meet me there. Don't start without me."

"I think I already have."

•••

As Avital walked away, Remo found a less-destroyed alcove and began punching numbers into the latest phone Smitty had given him. After a few minutes and a string of numbers rivaling pi, he smacked the side of it. "Why does it have to be so damned hard to dial Smitty?"

"Dialing: Smitty," an electronic voice within the phone said cheerily.

Remo looked at the screen of the phone, bemused. "Might've been useful if he'd told me it did that before," he said.

Smith's acrid voice came through the speaker as clearly as if he were there. "This isn't an authorized time."

"Yeah, I know, because the bad guys who've managed to crack your communications security don't go to lunch for another three hours, right?"

"What do you want, Remo?"

Remo hesitated, a sure indication to Smith that he wasn't going to like the news he was about to hear. "It's Chiun," Remo said. "I think he's sick." Remo could picture Smitty giving this fact its due reverence as the phone stayed silent. "He's just sits there watching the recordings of his soap operas."

"That sounds like any given day to me."

BULLY PULPIT

"It's more than just that," Remo said. "Something's affecting him. I think it's affecting me too, just not as badly. Maybe it's because he's more experienced or older or whatever." Remo struggled to explain how Chiun had fallen during the recent tremors, and what the Master of Sinanju had said right after about the pains of the Earth.

"Smitty, are we sure Silas Forben is dead, or do I owe you a refund?" Remo asked.

Smith coughed. Silas Forben had been an elderly scientist Remo encountered early in his career with CURE. Utilizing a unique invention he called a 'water laser,' he was able to activate fault lines—specifically the San Andreas Fault—and had attempted to use this capability to blackmail the U.S. Government. In the end Remo had killed him and pushed his assistants—his own daughters—into an open fissure which quickly closed over them. "The man known as Doctor Quake is very dead," Smith replied. "If you left any spark of life in him, I can guarantee the autopsy extinguished it."

"Anyone get their hands on his machines, or the blueprints?"

"Not likely," Smith said. "All the research was secured and the laboratory was swept clean."

"Well, it was worth a shot," Remo said. "Any news on these bad boys I'm trailing? Although, honestly Smitty, you're paying me for pretty much nothing. These guys are killing themselves without any help from me. I'm almost insulted."

"I'm working on that," Smith said. "I should know more soon. Meanwhile..." He paused, searching for the right words. "I'm sure Chiun will be fine. Probably just something in the water."

Remo rolled his eyes. "I'll relay your best wishes and condolences, Smitty."

• • •

When Avital turned a corner and was sure she was out of Remo's earshot, she took out her cellphone and entered the secure number to Ephraim.

"You can strike one operations center for ya Homaar," she said as soon as Ephraim picked up.

She could almost see Ephraim's befuddled expression as he tried to assimilate the terse message before he replied. "Explain yourself."

"The cell where I'd been meeting with Javid has been obliterated," she said. "Even the dust was shattered. And you won't guess who was on site when I arrived at the rubble."

"Do you think your Mr. Robespierre had something to do with it?"

Avital tried to think of alternatives. "Either he took it out, or he was coincidentally nearby when someone else did. And you know how I feel about coincidences," she said. "Of course, he claimed the latter."

"So you have not come into possession of one of the devices as yet."

She sighed. "It's frustrating," she said. "On the one hand,

our American agent is doing a damned fine job killing the enemy. But he's also blocking my efforts at finding a long term solution."

Avital could hear Ephraim's fingers tapping on the counter, a nervous habit he had when he was considering distasteful alternatives, which seemed to be all the time. "We should try to disable him, " he said. "Slow him down so you can get access to a device before he destroys the place."

She smiled, and the heat of it made Ephraim's cheek flush even over the phone.

"Exactly what I had in mind," she purred.

CHAPTER TEN

LA HAULE MANOR PRIDED ITSELF on the best, most extravagant cuisine its guests could imagine. The eager young waiter beamed with insouciant pride when the desirable Israeli reporter ordered the veal scaloppini with the saffron cream sauce and a bottle of vintage Rioja.

"And for the gentlemen?" he asked, beaming at Remo, who was hardly looking slovenly in his black turtleneck and tan chinos with matching jacket, but was decidedly underdressed contrasted to the lavender form-fitting gown that Avital had apparently painted on before coming down from her room.

Remo scanned down the menu, checking both sides, then checking the back. He finally zeroed in on the duck l'orange. "I'll have this," he said.

"An excellent choice, sir," the waiter beamed.

"But hold the l'orange," Remo added.

"Excuse me, sir?"

"Duck. But no sauce. And no seasoning. And…Oh, what the hell, it's a special occasion. You can bring the orange. Unpeeled."

The waiter blinked. "Just...the duck and an orange, sir?" He looked at Remo as though he had just ordered a plain hotdog from a five-star steakhouse.

"That'll do, gar-koney," he said. "Unless you have a nice white rice to go with it? It has to be cooked just right, though. And no seasoning on that, either."

The waiter took the menu and rolled his eyes. "I'm certain the chef will manage something, sir." He quickly marched into the kitchen, shaking his head and wondering how to tell their Le Cordon Bleu-trained chef that he was to prepare a plain duck on unseasoned white rice with an orange.

Avital didn't try to hide her amusement at the exchange. "You know, if you'd wanted Chinese, we could have gone to this lovely little place down the street from here."

"Oh, I can't stand Chinese," Remo said. "Who fries rice? All that grease. It's poison to the system."

"You're very health-conscious," she said, sipping her Rioja.

Remo patted his stomach. "Delicate constitution," he said.

"Now why do I think you're being less than forthcoming?" she purred, leaning in across the table.

"Honest Injun," Remo said, holding one hand up in the symbol of a solemn promise. "I was once hospitalized just from eating a hamburger." He sniffed his glass of water before determining it was clean enough to drink.

"So how is your friend? Chiun, I believe you called him?" she asked. "Feeling more himself?"

Remo grinned thinly. "He's acting more like his old self," he said. "I actually thought about cancelling our dinner to stay with him."

"Oh!" she exclaimed, her eyes widening a bit as she sat up a little straighter. "I didn't realize your relationship was..."

"No, no," Remo said. "It's nothing like that at all. He's the closest thing I've ever had to a father. Practically raised me to be the man I am today."

"Ah, I see," Avital responded, visibly relieved. But she couldn't truly understand just how complex was the bond between Remo and Chiun. Remo smiled fondly to himself as he recalled how he was introduced to the Master of Sinanju. He was given the news that he was going to be trained by the old man before him, and had been put quickly and painfully to sleep with an unseen hand after having called Chiun a "chink." It wasn't that Chiun minded the word; it was that Remo had insulted him by thinking him to be Chinese. Remo learned respect, of a kind, shortly thereafter, and Chiun had proceeded to cleanse his body and mind from the poisons of fast food and sloppy thinking, until Remo wasn't just the most efficient killing machine on the planet—he was the most efficient human organism alive today.

"He really is doing much better," Remo said. "When I left him, he literally was chasing me out of the room so that he could watch his soap operas in peace."

She laughed at the image of the ancient Korean cozied up in front of the television, entranced by the unbelievably complex storylines.

"Oh, don't do that," Remo warned. "He takes them very seriously. He even has working theories on how a fifty year old CEO can attend the wedding of his great-grandson who was just born a few years ago." She laughed again, musically. "He thinks they're the highest art form Western culture ever cobbled together."

"Which ones does he watch?" she asked. Remo was a bit embarrassed that he knew the names, and told her.

"Be thankful he doesn't speak Spanish," she said. "Telenovelas would absorb the rest of his world." This time it was Remo's turn to laugh. He didn't tell her that Chiun could speak Spanish, but simply chose not to involve himself in one of the "mongrel languages" unless he absolutely had no other choice.

The waiter returned with their food. Avital's was beautifully plated, with the saffron sauce artistically drizzled over the veal. To the side, there was a delicate pilaf, which had not been listed as part of the meal on the menu. In contrast, Remo's plate landed with an unceremonious *thunk* on the table, bearing a naked slice of duck breast, the orange rocking back and forth from the small impact with the table. To the side was a heaping pile of white rice, delivering the unmistakable message of what the chef thought about Remo's order.

In response, Remo sniffed the plate and wrinkled his nose.

"Is there a problem with the meal, sir?" the waiter asked, knowing full well there was indeed a problem with it, just not the one this American would recognize.

Remo sighed. "He salted the duck. Lightly, but he did it."

He forked at the rice, disheveling it a bit, then taking a nibble. "And he overcooked the rice. I thought you guys would have a good cook in a swanky joint like this."

"If you would like me to take the plate back..."

"And get the same plate back, with extra spit? No, thanks," Remo said. "This will be fine." Using his fork, he pushed the duck breast aside, into the rice, and began peeling the rind off the orange in a thin, continuous strip using his fingernail. "It's hard to screw up nature," he said as the waiter stalked away in a huff.

Avital shook her head in amused disbelief. "You know, this is why the French don't care much for Americans."

Remo laid the coiled rind in loops on his plate and pulled out a wedge of orange. "Poor service is why the Americans don't care much for the French," he said, popping the wedge into his mouth. "Among other reasons."

• • •

After dinner, Remo and Avital stepped out of the elevator, just one floor shy of the top and Remo's reserved floor of rooms. "I'm sorry for the mess," Avital said as she opened the door. "I was displaced from my penthouse room the other day. Some child of privilege bought out the whole upper floor, and so..." she spread her arms at the luggage that was hastily moved and stored.

"Don't apologize," Remo said. "I'm used to navigating around steamer trunks."

"Well, just find a seat...somewhere," she offered. "I'll be back in a bit." With that, she left the sitting area through the

French double-doors leading off to the bedroom, shutting them behind her. Remo paced idly through the room, looking at the two suitcases sitting side-by-side on the divan, the garment bag draped across the recliner, and three overnight bags occupying the length of the coffee table.

"You travel light," Remo said.

"You're teasing me, Mr. Robespierre," Avital called from behind the doors.

"No, really," Remo said. "You should see what I have to carry around when I'm on the road. Sure, there's no place to sit in here, but that's the hotel's fault for being so cramped."

The double doors opened, framing Avital's curvaceous figure, draped in a gauzy sunflower fabric masquerading as lingerie. She had undone her braid so that her hair spilled over both shoulders. "If you can't find a place to sit out there, you may want to look around in here," she murmured.

Remo didn't have to be asked twice. He stepped toward and through the French doors, and she stopped him with a hand on each of his shoulders. He paused, momentarily confused, until she began to push his jacket down his shoulders. Then he understood, allowing the jacket to slide down his arms and puddle on the floor. She liked to be in charge. Remo didn't have a problem with that at all.

"You barely had any dinner," Avital chided, as she began tugging the turtleneck out of Remo's pants and lifting it over his head, dropping it to the floor with his jacket. "You must be hungry," she said, running her fingertips down his bare chest.

"Ravenous," he growled, locking eyes with her before leaning in for the kiss. Their lips remained glued together as Avital fumbled with the buckle of his belt, popped the snap of his chinos and carefully lowered the zipper. Then both her hands were around him and gravity did the rest as Remo slipped out of his loafers and stepped out of the fallen pants. Gravity continued her gentle assistance, as though eager to join in, pulling the two downward onto the plush mattress.

It was fortunate that the bed was oversized. Within moments, Remo and Avital had found themselves conjoined, with each striving to be on top. Remo finally relented and allowed her to straddle his waist, and then her hand began to trace a nerve in his inner thigh along his femoral artery, sending a jolt of pleasure through him.

He was aware of the technique, but he had never put it into practice and never planned to. However, the knowledge of it was part of his Sinanju training. *This woman is a professional*, he realized, just as he also realized that this fact made her even more desirable.

"So who do you really work for?" she asked coyly, undulating her hips, inner muscles gripping him firmly as she gently rocked.

"Didn't we decide I was a reporter?" he asked, reaching forward and easily discarding the diaphanous lingerie. His eyes were drawn to her breasts as he made his own contribution to their carnal calisthenics.

She smirked, working the nerve in his inner thigh while reaching forward with her other hand to trace the perimeter of his pectoral muscle. "I think there's far more to you than that."

"So you thought you'd pump me for information?"

"Are you complaining?"

"Not in the slightest." He watched her slender hand wend its way down his body.

"Does it start with a C?" she teased playfully.

Remo shifted on the mattress, his only response a sheepish grin of admission.

She smiled wide, predatory and hungry, as her hand traced the outline of his abdominal muscles, taking the scenic route to its destination further south. "And is the second letter a vowel?" she continued. She punctuated her question with a small kiss on his chest.

"You know, you're pretty good at this," Remo said. "I bet you never lost a game of hangman." He gently took her wrist and began stroking the length of her forearm, feeling the beat of her pulse quickening at the touch.

Avital felt a tingling through her body and strove to ignore it. "And is…" She paused, gasped, and began again. "And is the last letter also a vowel?" she rasped out. Things were getting more heated than she anticipated. *What is it about this American*, she wondered as her mind began to fog, *that affects me so? He's not the most handsome man. His face is drawn, gaunt—it's almost like a skull. And yet…*

Remo feigned astonishment. "As a matter of fact, it is," he said, as his body continued to mass-produce masculine hormones. His fingers were lightly tapping their way further up her inner forearm. "Do they teach you how to do that in the Mossad or is it a natural talent?"

"In what?" She swooned, her eyes rolling back. She began rocking faster, bouncing harder. Her body was acting first and choosing to tell her brain what had been done after the fact.

"You know," he said, pushing up against her. "The Israeli spy agency?"

"I..." His fingers began exploring the sides of her breasts, his thumbs on her nipples. "Yes," she admitted. And then she admitted it a dozen more times, each time a little bit louder than the last confession, as Remo learned all about ya Homaar.

• • •

Much later, Avital laid back against a mound of pillows, with the back of Remo's head nuzzled between her breasts. Her willowy arms draped around his shoulders, tracing his strong forearms, from his elbows to his wrists.

"They're so thick," she said.

"Product of a misspent youth," Remo said airily. "I didn't date much as a teenager." He removed his wrist from her gentle grasp to stroke the side of one her breasts.

"That explains one wrist," she teased.

"I'm ambidextrous." And using his other hand, he began to trace the outer edge of her other breast.

"So," she giggled, combing her fingers through his hair. "You like my tits, huh?"

Remo looked up at her. "That depends," he said. "Is Mahtits another one of those ya Homaar goons? If not, then I'm going to go with a yes."

BULLY PULPIT

She gave a small laugh, and wrapped her arms around his waist, massaging him back to full alertness. He let her fingers work their magic, resting his head between the two pillows nature provided her. He closed his eyes.

And a wave passed through his body, sending his balance reeling. A flush overtook his senses, and he felt momentarily as though his brains were going to drain out his mouth. He reached out his arms, grasping at the sheet to steady himself, just as the sensation subsided.

"Everything all right?" Avital asked.

Remo shuddered. "I think I just felt the Earth move," he said.

She kissed his cheek. "You're welcome."

• • •

Remo pressed the button for the elevator, then waited for Avital's door to close before walking to the stairs and sprinting up to the next floor. He needed to talk with Chiun about the disconnectedness he experienced, and he was worried that it must have been even worse for the ancient master of Sinanju.

"Little Father," he said, entering the room where Chiun still sat lotus-style on the floor in front of the television. The device was tuned into an international weather channel, where a very excited gentleman in a rumpled suit was talking rapidly.

"We've never seen activity like this before, Bryan," he said to his off-screen partner. "In just the past hour, we've had tremors in Saint Louis, California, Mexico City, and

Japan, ranging from 3.5 to an astonishing 5.2—in Montana, of all places!"

The camera cut over to a serious-looking man in his early forties. "Joe, is it possible that all this earthquake activity is the result of fracking? Is Mother Earth finally telling us to get our act together and stop raping and pillaging her natural resources?"

Joe coughed. "Well, it's really hard to say at this point what's causing all this activity, Bryan," he said. "But it's certainly going to be interesting finding out. We're getting a report now that a mild tremor has even been felt in Iraq, near Baghdad."

"That's got to be hard for those poor people," Bryan said. "I've been over there, you know, when the helicopter I was in got hit by..."

Remo turned the set off and squatted by Chiun. "Little Father," he repeated. Chiun sat still, peaceful as ever, his wizened face more at rest than Remo had ever seen it before, his vellum eyelids fully closed. Normally, Chiun responded immediately to Remo walking in with some cutting observation or guilt-laden lament. That he remained still frightened Remo to his core.

He put his hands on Chiun's shoulders gently, taking his life in his hands to give him the slightest shake.

Chiun did not wake up.

CHAPTER ELEVEN

HAROLD W. SMITH HAD A HEADACHE. He now knew the intimate details of everyone who worked at the headquarters for Billy Walker's Evangelical Outreach Ministries. Their personnel files, their credit reports, and their online purchases were all organized and collated within the CURE computer banks, and none revealed anything remotely incriminating. From the front receptionist to the chief financial officer, all had impeccable records. Perhaps Walker knew he'd be scrutinized forever after the incident with the reporter from *The Clarion*, and extended that caution to his hiring practices?

Most frustrating was the lack of any electronic calendar entry that would show who the ya Homaar representative went to see. Not that it was all that surprising. Meeting with someone like Abdel Kassab, a member of a terrorist organization, is something one would want to keep out of any potential paper trail.

The reporter's death kept nagging at him. Smith's brought up the file on Jake Riser once more, looking over the crime photos and the digital evidence locker. His attention again was drawn to the numbers scrawled with the dead man's blood. *1:49*. What did it mean, though? He'd already ruled out time of death, as it was determined that the mugging/murder had happened later than that, and it didn't make sense that the dying man's last message was one intended just to help the M.E. in his analysis.

It occurred to him that perhaps the numbers were a scriptural reference. He'd been investigating a ministerial organization, after all; it would make sense. With a few taps of the keyboard, Smith brought up displays of all the biblical references with chapter one and verse forty-nine. He was surprised there were so few.

If they meant anything at all, Smith couldn't see it, but at this point he couldn't rule anything out. Perhaps they might mean something to someone else. He didn't think the Numbers reference was important ("*Only thou shalt not number the tribe of Levi, neither take the sum of them among the children of Israel*"), nor the scriptures from I Kings ("*And all the guests that were with Adonijah were afraid, and rose up, and went every man his way*") or I Chronicles ("*And when Shaul was dead, Baalhanan the son of Achbor reigned in his stead*").

So much for the Old Testament. The New Testament had a few that looked more promisingly laudatory, however. Luke offered "*For he that is mighty hath done to me great things; and holy is his name*," while John topped that with "*Nathanael answered and saith unto him, Rabbi, thou art the Son of God; thou art the King of Israel.*" Either one might sound good to shout while crashing a plane into a building or a mountain, but they were a bit wordy to be a motto. And neither of them carried anything that Smith could determine to resemble anything like a clue.

Smitty put the system to work pulling up complete histories of both Jacob Riser and Billy Walker. Perhaps they'd crossed paths sometime between the lawsuit and Riser's death.

Riser's history was short. After the Chicago lawsuit, he'd popped up in California several months later. This was a few years before Walker set up his operation, so it wasn't an issue of stalking. Riser had taken on a position with a tabloid, writing under an assumed name and largely writing fictional news pieces. His work had come a long way down. From his exposé on the Cradle Robber serial killer, his work had devolved into stories about apocalyptic signs found in tacos, invisible men who could walk through walls, and a hidden tribe of anthropomorphic tiger-people living in Middlesex Fells—hackery no sane person would ever find credible. None of his articles mentioned Walker in any capacity, although it was clear Riser had never given up on that story.

Walker's own history was more copious. After the money began pouring in, Walker lived up to the merciful and forgiving image the country saw. He did more than just manage a ministry; he put his money to work creating American jobs. With friends he made in Congress, he was able to easily get permits for oil drilling operations around the country, employing hundreds of Americans. Despite the potential windfalls he stood to reap, Walker had recently sold off the operation to an outfit from Texas, and had plowed his money into two more job-creating ventures: strip mining and urban renewal. The unions loved him, as he created employment for miners and construction workers. The digital history included two headlines about derelict buildings that had been scheduled for demolition that prior week, urging viewers to tune in to webcam broadcasts so they could watch these eyesores tumble to the ground.

The announced time of one of the demolitions struck Smith curiously. Why did that date and time sound familiar to him? Then he knew where he'd seen it, and brought up the image of the printed spreadsheet Riser's body had covered. One of the dates and times on the list corresponded exactly with that demolition. Smith quickly checked the other. It didn't show on Riser's list—until Smith allowed for the time zone difference. Sure enough, it was on the list.

Why would Riser be carrying a list of construction kickoffs? And why would he be killed over them? He cross-checked the rest of the times with Walker's public schedule of renovations, but nothing matched. Smith didn't believe the alignment of the two times were coincidental, so what did the other ones on the list signify? His fingers flew over the keyboard, and he brought up the timetables for the mining operations, including planned detonations. Two of those detonations, adjusted for time zones, fit neatly into Riser's list. But why?

There was something else about the list, something he hadn't noticed before, but he couldn't quite put his finger on it.

The phone rang—the special phone—and Smith's headache grew worse.

"We need to have a discussion about these unscheduled calls," Smith said into the phone without salutation.

"Smitty, I need help!"

Smith felt his heart skip a beat. Remo was the one Smith went to when he needed help. Whenever Remo needed help from him, things had gotten just about as bad as they could.

"Smitty! I need you to tell this doctor not to administer any drugs to Chiun," Remo insisted. "This nut's going to kill him."

Smith wondered for a half a second why Chiun wasn't the one killing the nut. "I need more information."

"Later, just stop him."

Smith heard the phone being passed over, and a European voice came on the line.

"Is this *Doctor* Harold Smith?" the voice asked questioningly.

"It is," Smith answered. "What seems to be the problem?"

"Is Mr. Parks your patient?"

Smith cleared his throat. "I see to his care, yes."

"Dr. Smith, Mr. Parks was brought to us in a comatose condition. His vitals are alarmingly low, his breathing is shallow, his heartbeat is barely detectable," said the man across the ocean. "All I'm trying to do is give him some basic antibiotics to stave off infections, plus nutrients to prevent malnutrition. His friend, this maniac, continues to prevent me from doing my job."

"Smitty, I swear to God, I'll break his arms off," Remo yelled in the background.

"Who am I speaking with?" Smith asked.

"Doctor Tavis Munro, with Island Medical Centre," he answered. "I'm sorry, I should have introduced myself. It's just that I'm a bit flustered at all this."

"I understand your frustration, Dr. Munro," Smith said. "Dr. Munro, Mr. Parks has a very delicate condition. There are very few medications he can take that won't end up killing him."

Munro paused. "What sort of condition?"

"I'll send over his paperwork," Smith said. "In the meantime, administer nothing but hydration."

The other doctor sighed. "I'll do that for now, but I need to see his history as soon as possible."

"Understood," Smith said. "Please put the young man back on the phone before you begin."

Before Remo could start in, Smith assured him nothing more than basic saline solution would be given to Chiun.

"And you think this happened to Chiun because of earthquakes?" Smith asked after Remo explained how he had found Chiun comatose before his television set.

"I'm certain Chiun believed it," Remo said. "And I've got to tell you, Smitty, I'm starting to feel like the third time around the tilt-a-whirl myself. What the hell is going on?"

Smith pursed his lips, his face pinching into a look of constipation. "I don't know," Smith said. "But we'll find out."

Smith hung up the phone and turned back to the computer. Much as Remo's situation concerned him, there was precious little CURE could do to prevent natural disasters, even if they were occurring in more frequent intervals.

Intervals! Smith cursed himself for having missed the obvious—simple mathematics. He subtracted one time from the next, and had his answer. Just to be certain, he went down the entire list. Without fail, adjusting each date and time into the same time zone, the answer came up the same. Each event was happening at a consistent interval.

Exactly one hour and forty-nine minutes apart.

But what did it mean? Smith knew he'd stumbled upon an important piece of a puzzle, but he still didn't have the picture he was supposed to construct. He went back to the CURE main screen, staring intently into the construct, that floating digital model of a molecule, as if the answer were somewhere to be gleaned from the floating bits and bytes.

Sprouting from the ya Homaar cluster like buds on a tree, two more notices of earthquakes appeared. Smith shook his head. It was just a little bit ago he had moved yet another report about an earthquake into the trash. Could it be that he'd been wrong all along, that the CURE system was actually reporting a valid threat?

He opened the wastebasket and restored the earthquake stories to the data mine. The visible results were dramatic. No longer were there a cluster of various sized threats interconnected on a three-dimensional floating wireframe. Now there was only one threat, one pulsating sphere, dominating the entirety of the screen. The computer had indeed identified a threat, and had even assigned a name to who was behind it. Unfortunately, that man had been dead for almost a hundred years.

CHAPTER TWELVE

RAY STANFORD'S EYES WENT WIDE behind his red-rimmed glasses, and his voice went up in octaves with each uttered phrase. "Nikola Tesla? Father of Alternating Current? Inventor of the first electric car, wireless transmission of energy, and the death ray?"

Ray was tall and slender, dressed in a tweed jacket over a navy turtleneck. Offsetting his conservative academic appearance were the rims of his eyeglasses, which were a neon red that matched the oversized plastic watchband he wore with the comic book superhero emblem on the face. The statement was, "I may be a professor, but I retain my geek cred."

"Death ray?" Smith repeated. He had only moments ago greeted the Saint John's University adjunct professor with a dead-fish handshake that had been reciprocated in kind by the wiry African-American geologist. Smith had driven the 25 miles from Rye, which took the better part of an hour as he avoided the tolls, to secure a personal meeting with the man, and was already feeling that the effort might have been a wasted one.

"You bet!" Ray said. "Imagine a gun that emits electricity or microwave energy. I mean, that's no different from your TV remote, really—which Tesla also invented! What else could you call something like that?" Ray began talking faster the more he got into his subject. "Of course, the government shut all that down, commandeered all his work and locked it up at Wright-Patterson Air Force Base—along with all that UFO technology." He gave Smith a lopsided grin to indicate he was being facetious about the UFOs, unaware that Smith was immune to humor in any form.

"Did he do any work with earthquakes?" Smith asked. When he allowed the CURE computer to finally consider the numerous earthquake reports, it pointed unerringly to the eccentric inventor. He found that Stanford operated a computer website dedicated to paranormal trivia, which included several references to Tesla—so many, in fact, that it was apparent Tesla was the geologist's favorite focus.

"Oh, yes," Ray said with enthusiasm. "The Great Street Earthquake," he added with a nod. Getting no response from Smith, he continued. "See, Tesla had been fiddling around in his basement with a motor no more powerful than your basic push mower. He fixed it to a beam mounted in the floor and monitored it to see if he could find the beam's frequency by raising and lowering the vibrations. He made huge strides in the science of mechanical resonance. You know what that is, right?"

"Yes," Smith replied, nodding.

"Basically, resonance is the tendency of an object, or a system, to oscillate with greater amplitude at some frequencies than others," Ray continued pedantically, ignoring Smith's statement. "If I bombard a rock with a frequency of 20 Megahertz, it will vibrate at a certain rate. If I hit it with 30 Megahertz, it will vibrate at a different rate. With trial and error, you eventually find the resonant frequency of the object, when the frequency causes the object to vibrate the fastest."

"The greater the frequency, the greater the vibration," Smith said drily. "So what?"

"Well, it's not just that," Ray said. "You can overshoot the frequency and not hit the resonance of the object. It's the same principle behind soldiers breaking step when they walk over a bridge."

Smith nodded. Finally the academic had used an allegory he could relate to. "Because marching in step causes the bridge to vibrate," Smith said, nodding.

"And maybe even *break apart*!" Ray grinned, glad to see he was reaching his new pupil. "You've seen opera singers break a wineglass with their voice? Mechanical resonance is pretty much the same thing, only the system in question is a...well, a mechanical one."

"A machine."

"Well, not necessarily something man-made," Ray said, removing his glasses for a quick polish before pushing them back into place. "Any system that involves force and movement could be considered a mechanical system. Anyway, while Tesla wasn't making much progress in his basement with that steel beam, outside, store windows up and down the street were shaking and shattering like an earthquake was happening. The police were called, and he shut off the motor. It was an accident, but later he tried it again intentionally on a building under construction, and in just a few minutes he reported that the structure started to wobble. Another ten minutes and he could have brought it down. He claimed he could drop the whole Brooklyn Bridge in less than an hour doing that if he wanted."

Ray's energy was causing his glasses to steam up again with sweat. "But it was his plans for the wireless transmission of energy that was the really cool stuff," he continued. "Nobody believed him, though—or they believed him and worked to discredit him. Edison had friends in high places."

"So he could tear anything apart, just by shaking it the right way?" Smith said, trying to steer the conversation back on track. "No matter how big? Even, say, planet-sized?"

Ray coughed politely. "Planet-sized, sir? Oh, you must be thinking of The Great Scare!" He seemed to have a book title for every misadventure in Tesla's biography. "He caused quite a panic with that theory! A thousand pounds of dynamite set off about every two hours, and he said he could crack the Earth like a boy cracks an egg—in just a few months."

"Do you think he was right?"

"About the timing and forces necessary?" Ray shrugged. "Probably. The man never gave out a number unless he was absolutely sure. But he also said it couldn't be done because nobody could accurately plot the peaks and ebbs of the Earth's periodicity."

"That was then, though," Smith said. "Do you think someone could do it today?"

Ray steepled his index fingers and tapped them against his chin, the vibrations of which sent his vermillion-rimmed spectacles sliding down the bridge of his nose. "It'd be an interesting experiment," he said. His voice began to trail off as he began talking more to himself than Smith, already drawing up the tests in his head. "I suppose it could be done, given enough resources. It would be extremely expensive. You'd have to set up a number of drilling sites all over the world…"

"Drilling sites?" Smith said. "Like oil wells?"

"Exactly," Ray nodded enthusiastically. "Oil drills would be perfect, so long as they didn't actually *find* any oil," he added bitterly.

If Smith had pursed his lips together any tighter, they would have merged. He had selected Ray Stanford from a list of candidates based on grant applications. "Fascinating," he said. "Maybe someone will get us those statistics someday. And speaking of oil, that brings me to the real purpose of my visit."

"I *was* wondering why the Department of Conservation was interested in my blog," Ray said nervously. "You post enough government conspiracies, you start to believe some of them and expect to get a visit."

Smith gave a thin-lipped smile that probably reinforced any belief Stanford had in aliens as he reached inside his jacket and retrieved a manila envelope, "Nothing so dramatic," he said. "You applied for a grant a while back to study the effects of fracking on the aquifer systems of South Dakota."

Ray's eyes widened. "Well, yes, but that was declined some time back."

"It's been reconsidered," Smith said, forcing a smile. "Will one hundred and fifty get you started?"

"One hundred and fifty *thousand*?" Ray couldn't believe his luck as he took the envelope from Smith and counted the zeroes on the bank draft inside, evaporating most of the idle conversation that had just enjoyed about Tesla and mechanical resonance and oil drilling.

"We think you can do your country a valuable service," Smith said honestly. "Go forth and research."

Smith started for the door. "Thank you!" Ray called after him, as if startling awake from a dream. "Hey, I wasn't kidding about that death ray stuff. He tried to tell folks he could transmit unlimited power without wires and they laughed at him. He said he'd show them all the true power of it and disappeared. Three days later? Boom! Tunguska!"

"I thought that was a meteor strike," Smith said, his hand resting on the doorknob.

"Meteor strikes leave meteor fragments," Ray grinned, staring down at his new financing. "Check it out sometime."

• • •

All the drive back to Rye, New York, Smith mulled over information. He realized he could have called Professor Stanford for the information, but he wanted to make sure the conversation was forgotten, and money was the great amnesiac. Now, as he sat at his desk back at Folcroft Sanitarium, he was beginning to wonder if he had made a mistake—if perhaps he did not have the time to be wasting. His stomach was curdling. If his suspicions panned out, he could not even consider the ramifications, particularly if the world found out.

It was Stanford's hypothesis about using oil well exploration that had nearly clinched it for him, but there were still too many holes left in the pattern.

Or maybe there weren't that many holes after all. Maybe he just was not considering all the viable options.

Smith took a cleansing breath and picked up the phone. To his surprise, it was answered on the first ring.

"Not really a great time, Smitty," Remo said. "I'm making them take Chiun back to La Haule, and they're not real happy about it."

"I'll make the arrangements, Remo," Smith said. "But I need to know something. What time did those explosions happen?"

"Both of them?" Remo asked. "The first one just before lunch. The other closer to three in the afternoon."

"Can you be more precise?"

"More precise? 11:32 AM and 3:09 PM," Remo stated. "Give or take ten seconds."

Smith looked for the opportunities he didn't want to see, and saw them. Adjusting for time zones, both explosions fit precisely into Jake Riser's spreadsheet of times. The explosions weren't just happening with frequency, they were happening on a schedule. Mechanical resonance—on a global scale.

"Remo, things are worse than we thought," Smith said.

CHAPTER THIRTEEN

"THIS IS NOT HOW THIS WAS SUPPOSED TO WORK!" Achmed spoke loudly into the microphone plugged into his ten-year-old desktop computer. The power cable had just been taped back together after one of the wandering goats had decided to snack on it, delivering what proved to be a convenient method for quick-roasting goats, and also teaching the ya Homaar operatives a lesson about keeping your wires bundled and protected.

The voice coming through the dual cube speakers had an after-echo which annoyed Achmed to no end because he didn't realize his microphone was in front of his speakers. Every sound that came out went back into the microphone and was carried through the system again, causing everything to repeat. "The deal was for free bombs," said a decidedly female voice. "We give them to you, and you blow them up where you said you would, when we told you to."

Achmed spoke slowly, carefully, and more loudly than necessary directly into the microphone. "But the bombs, they are too—" he struggled for the word 'volatile' before deciding on "—explodey. They are killing our members."

An echoing giggle came from the speakers. "They're

suicide bombers, right?" she said. "They're supposed to die."

"Yes, but they're supposed to be sending a message with their death!" Achmed sputtered. He raised his hands in frustration. In the back of the cave they used as a headquarters, Akbar was finishing up his portion of electrocuted goat. He looked up from his meal and shrugged his shoulders, as if to say, "You get what you pay for."

"We did tell you that you were expected to adhere to a tight schedule," the woman warned. "If your men are incapable of telling time then your problems will only continue. You still have over a hundred of the vests undetonated."

Achmed took a deep breath, filling his nostrils with the scent of goat manure. Along the rock ledge against which his computer station was positioned, a rat nosed its way along, dislodging pebbles as it foraged for something to eat and leaving a trail of droppings in its passing.

"It is not that we are not grateful," Achmed replied. "But if we can't budge our schedules even the slightest, then why teach our men how to use the detonator?"

More giggles poured out of the speakers. "Those aren't detonators, baby," she laughed. "Those are confidence props. Hand-held courage. The magic feather that lets the elephant fly."

"Elephant fly?" Akbar asked from the back of the cave. He wiped goat grease from his chin, boggling at how Americans could have become such a world superpower and yet be so insane as to believe in flying elephants. Or did they actually have flying elephants? Who knew what kinds of things the scientists in American laboratories could put together?

"It's easier to get someone to blow themselves up if they believe they're the ones pressing the button," she said. "But make no mistake, Mister Achmed, each of those bombs will blow up when we told you they would. So if you have any kind of statement you want to make, I'd start using recruits with more punctuality." More giggling bubbled through the speakers before the system began to sputter, preceded by a painful squeak of the rat whose freshly spewed urine had just penetrated the loosely wrapped tape around the computer's electrical cable, frying both him and the computer at the same time.

• • •

In a repurposed warehouse, under a cold, gunmetal gray sky, the Reverend Billy Walker knelt in front of a leather couch. His elbows pressed into the cushions, and his clasped hands provided a resting place for his forehead, as he continued to shake the gates of Heaven with his prayers.

"Oh Lord," he cried out in his solitude. "Where art thou, and where art the sounds of thine trumpets?" Walker's cheeks were reddened with tears. "*And great earthquakes shall be in divers places, and famines, and pestilences; and fearful sights and great signs shall there be from heaven.*" Walker frequently quoted scripture in his prayers, a habit he had been taught by his own childhood pastor, to "pray the word." "Father, You have told us Your word would not return void. Well, Lord, I have prayed Your words unto You, and I have put works to my faith so that it is shown to be alive. I have said unto this mountain we call Earth, 'Be thou removed!'"

As he moaned from his soul, two women silently entered his chambers. They were dressed identically in white slacks and blouses, and their hair was pulled back severely in tight buns. They knelt on each side of him, careful not to disturb him, folding their hands in the semblance of prayer as they cut their eyes at each other and grinned.

"Father, I have seen to it that the mountain shall be removed. But I still do not see the signs of Your coming."

The girl on his left bit her lip to stifle a giggle.

"But I hold out hope, Lord," he prayed. "For without this hope, we would be of all men most miserable. Still, even so, come quickly, Lord. I long for Your returning, for the sake of the elect. Show us Your power and grace through the promise of Your glorious returning, I pray. Amen."

The girls' smirks were instantly wiped to passive expressions of tranquility as the Reverend Walker pulled a handkerchief from his pocket, wiped his forehead and cheeks, and blew his nose. "Oh, hello, girls," he said. "I didn't hear you come in."

"We didn't want to disturb you, Reverend Billy," said the one to his left. She touched his shoulder gently. "All is well. We have spoken with our customer, and they have seen the light."

Walker wiped at his nose and sat down on the sofa with a sigh. "I only hope it's enough," he said. "I was moved to prayer after a phone call from one of my foremen."

"A phone call?" It was the second girl, speaking more sharply than she ever had to the Reverend before. "Billy, I thought we made it clear that there could be no communication. People in power can find you through your phone. You were supposed to leave it in California."

Walker nodded. "I know, I know," he said. "And you're right. But I needed to know if things changed, and they have." He sighed. "I believe someone has figured out my mission."

"Why do you say that?" asked the first girl. Her lips formed a slight pout, and worry wrinkles marred the alabaster skin of her forehead. "The reporter died before he had a chance to tell anybody what he knew."

"Nevertheless," Walker said, "I've just been informed that the urban renewal in Detroit has been halted due to unexpected changes in the zoning ordinances."

"That's why we have a backup plan," the second girl said.

"And the EPA has put a halt to the strip mining in West Virginia because someone phoned in that they saw a certain species of woodpecker in the area," he added. "And the Mexican government has actually returned our incentive money and refused any further demolition efforts in Guadalajara."

The girls paused, taking this in. "The backup plan is still viable," the second one said. "The plan is far enough in motion."

"Even if all our operations have been stopped? Because it's certainly looking like that's what has happened." Walker looked at them hopefully. It was his dream, but it had been their science that had brought that dream close to reality. He had put as much faith and trust in them as he had in God—perhaps even more, since they had come through on their promises more frequently and more recently.

"Even if," the second girl confirmed. She leaned in and kissed his cheek, her breasts lightly swaying braless in her blouse as she did. "We've nearly reached the tipping point," she promised. "In a few more days, the process will be irreversible, even if we never detonated another bomb after that."

Reverend Walker's face radiated hope at hearing her words. "Thank you," he gushed. "For everything." He clasped both of their hands in his. "I only pray that our Lord will have mercy on you both when he returns. Your service is to me, but the sin is all mine, and should rest on my shoulders." With that, he turned and left them in the makeshift office that had been waiting for him on their arrival, ambling down the echoing hallways, singing a hymn to himself. *"He's coming soon. He's coming soon. With joy we welcome his return-ing."*

The sisters looked at each other. "It will work, won't it?" the first one asked.

"You always were such a doubter," the second replied, as she ran her fingers through her sister's jet-black locks. "Trust the science. We're about to make the final chapter of history."

The first girl giggled. "Science is sexy," she said, taking her sister's hand.

CHAPTER FOURTEEN

REMO WILLIAMS HAD SEEN more than his fair share of weirdness in his career with CURE, but every once in awhile he could still find something that surprised him. As Smitty tried to explain to him the source of the earthquakes, and where they were ultimately headed, Remo nodded his head, cycling his hand through the air in a silent and unseen urge for Smitty to get through the explanation. Remo already understood the principle Smitty was describing—minimized expenditure of energy for maximum impact. Sinanju was all about that principle.

"Yeah, yeah, yeah, I got it, Smitty," Remo said, interrupting Smith's briefing. "Just point me at who I have to kill."

Smith cleared his throat. "Well, that is part of the problem," he said. "I don't know who it is."

"Smitty, you wouldn't be calling me if you didn't know," Remo said. "At the very least you've got an idea."

"I have narrowed down the pool of suspects, yes," Smith admitted. "I am certain that it is someone inside the Billy Walker organization." He explained how someone in the hierarchy had met with ya Homaar, and how only someone with authority could have controlled the schedule of detonations in the renovation and strip mining projects—projects that Smitty had now paralyzed by tying them up in bureaucratic red tape.

"Smitty, you've lied to me more times than I can count since I started with CURE," Remo said. "But I do believe this is the first time I've ever heard you lie to yourself."

"I don't know what you mean."

"You want to think someone in the palatial parsonage is controlling the detonations and meeting with terrorists," Remo said. "But who do you think could make the final decision to get out of the oil drilling business and set up those other enterprises in the first place?"

Remo's question was met with silence.

"I think we both know there's only one person who could make those decisions, and exercise that level of control," said Remo. "So all you have to do is tell me where I can find Billy Walker."

More silence. "I can't do that," Smitty finally replied.

"You can't? Or you won't?"

"I can't," he said. "Not without making a phone call first."

• • •

In the Oval Office, a phone buzzed, startling the man who worked there. "Hello?" he answered tentatively.

"Mr. President."

The President sniffed. "Dr. Smith," he said. "Are you calling to tender your resignation? You know, just because you removed your special direct line to my office doesn't mean I can't have your little organization disbanded. I've got a pen and I've got a…another phone, and I could put you out of business like that." Smith heard two soft thwips followed by one solid snap.

"If you wish, Mr. President," Smith continued. "But there's a situation that I can't move forward on without your authorization."

In short order, Smith told the President of the United States that not only was there someone out there with the capability to destroy the world, and that this someone was already well down the path to making it a reality. He told the President that this person was working with the terrorists, ya Homaar, and the role they played—knowingly or not—in the man's master plan.

"Are you asking me to ask you to send that man after him?"

"I am, sir."

"Who is the target?"

Smith cleared his throat. "It's the Reverend Billy Walker, sir."

Smith could hear the President breathing on the other end of the phone as the information sank in. "Dr. Smith, do you really believe this?" he asked. "What possible motivation would America's Pastor have to kill billions of people? He just officiated at the White House prayer breakfast two months ago!"

"I understand that, sir," Smith said. "I don't know why he is planning this either." After a pause, he added, "My wife, she owned several recordings of his concerts."

"Dr. Smith, I cannot in good conscience ask you to send that man after the Reverend Walker," the President said.

"Nevertheless, sir, the situation needs to be handled," Smith said. "You could send in another agency, but it would involve more manpower. Invariably, someone would ask why they were taking the mission. Inevitably, someone would learn the procedures involved in the destruction. And the more people who learn the process, the greater the chance that someone will reproduce the procedure—someone smarter, someone harder to pin down. Basically, sir, someone who would succeed."

"You honestly believe someone would try to destroy the world?" the President asked after several seconds. "Isn't that just a little too sci-fi?"

"I don't want to believe it, sir," Smith said. "But I don't get to pick which facts I like and which facts I don't."

There was more silence from the Oval Office.

"Mr. President," Smith prodded. "I need your permission."

• • •

Remo sat at attention in a wooden-backed chair positioned beside the hospital bed that had been set up in their suite of rooms. Chiun lay there, his wizened face ashen, his high forehead mottled, his wispy hair and beard looking scraggly and limp. He had never looked older.

A nurse had been assigned to stay with Chiun as well, to monitor his heartbeat and change the saline bag that kept him hydrated. In a previous life, she was the kind of nurse Remo would be charming into an after-hours tryst, but now his mind was focused on one thing: finding the son of a bitch who had put Chiun in this state—this idiot who wanted to blow up the planet like some cartoon Martian—and shoving a little Sinanju up his ass. He didn't know how that was going to stop the world from shaking apart, but it would sure make him feel better.

As Remo expected the phone to ring, he was momentarily startled by a knock at the door. He let the nurse go to check it. It was probably for her anyway, since neither he nor Chiun had told anyone they were staying here.

Avital glided quickly into the room toward Remo. Her hair was loose and flowing, and her body was wrapped in a gauzy sky-blue sundress with thin little straps over her shoulders. "Why didn't you tell me you were—" She stopped short when she saw the medical equipment, the tubes and wires, all connected to the shriveled little Asian man in a portable bed. "Oh my God," she said, rushing to Chiun's side. "What happened?"

Remo stood and walked to her side. "Coma," he said without elaborating. Seeing her expression, he added, "He has food allergies."

"Food allergies?" she repeated, shocked. "Is he going to be all right?"

Remo searched himself for a flippant response, but came up dry. He shrugged. Avital had been prepared to read Remo the riot act, having discovered that he and Chiun were the ones who had dispossessed her of her former room, but she was unprepared for the scene she had stumbled on.

The two of them stood there in awkward silence. Finally, Avital spoke up. "I'm leaving."

"Okay. Dinner later?"

"No, I mean I'm leaving Jersey," she said. "There's another cell operating out of Syria. It's not as glamorous, but…"

"But that's the biz," Remo answered, knowing.

"That is, as you say, the biz," she said.

The phone rang. Remo looked at the display and answered. "Uncle Charlie, thank you for the birthday card."

Smith recognized the phrase and knew Remo wasn't alone. "Your Aunt Rose says you should spend the money on whatever you want," he answered, which Remo understood to mean that permission had been obtained to move forward.

"Where is she," he asked, stepping into the next room away from Avital. "I'd like to give her my love."

"I don't know where she's gone at the moment," Smith replied. It was true. He didn't know where Billy Walker was. The man had disappeared off the face of the planet. Given the situation, perhaps literally. Smith had seen more far-fetched things in his time as the director of CURE.

"That's okay," Remo said, glancing at Avital. "I've heard where her sewing circle is meeting. I'll try her there. But I can't leave my friend just yet. Not in this condition."

Smith paused. "I understand. If you leave him, he might die. But if you don't leave him…"

Remo sighed. "Then he definitely will."

"Let me know what you find."

"Will do," Remo said with faked cheerfulness. "Take care, Uncle Charlie."

He hung up the phone. "So," he said. "Syria."

"Yes," she said. "I'll be leaving in the morning."

"What's wrong with tonight?"

For a split second she thought he was rushing her away. The thought of it pained her—something she was not used to feeling. Normally she was the one walking away from a mess of a man. Looking at Remo, she felt like she was the mess, and that was the most desirable kind of discomfort she had ever experienced. But when she saw the set of his jaw, and the intensity in his deep-set eyes, so dark they were nearly black, she knew it was more than that.

"Are you coming with me, Mr. CIA man?" she asked, her eyebrows arching, a blush coming to her cheek with the anticipation of spending time alone with this strange man who threw people like paper airplanes and melted her knees with a glance.

Remo cut his eyes to the prone, frail body of Chiun. The monitor tracking his heart rate gave a blip. It took far too long to give another one.

"Try to stop me," he said with an edge of bitterness. He knew it wasn't a direct line to Walker, but it might get him one step closer to the man who had put Chiun into this coma. "Let me know where we're going, then go pack. I'll have a plane ready and waiting."

CHAPTER FIFTEEN

MOHAMMAD IBN MOHAMMAD AL ISLAM sat by the window in his room, looking out at the crumbling structure across the street. He was a patient man, a cunning man, and his talents had helped him rise quickly through the ranks of Daesh. It helped that he had been born in Connecticut as James Beckworth III, and attended Harvard.

He had taken his post-graduate trust fund from his parents and immediately set off to France for what he said would be a well-deserved celebration of his accomplishment. However, shortly thereafter, he made contact with recruiters from Daesh who helped him realize his dream of bringing death to America for all the evils it wrought on the world. Oh, America had its minor advantages, like allowing people to acquire enough wealth to send their children to Ivy League schools. But it also oppressed countries that stood for all the things James Beckworth III—now Mohammad ibn Mohammad al Islam—believed in, such as bedding 14-year-old girls and executing gays. America had to be taken out of the way.

In between filming videos for Daesh (because his voice

was strident and his vocabulary erudite), he trained with weapons until he was adequate with a pistol. More than adequate, in fact: his years as a youth spent shooting skeet with his father at the country club had honed his eye. He had only needed to overcome the reluctance to pull the trigger when the target was a human being.

He remembered the first time. It took him three minutes, and then they told him the victim was gay. He still felt a rush when he thought about the way the blood flowed out of the eyes and nostrils after the bullet went up through the chin, like a crimson fountain.

Now he had the opportunity to prove the superiority of Daesh to an upstart insurgent movement that had broken away from the fold. The ya Homaar were negligible for a long time, but recently they had managed to get their hands on some explosive technology that was well beyond their own means to create or control. These weapons would be put to much better use in the hands of the skilled freedom fighters of Daesh. Through friends of friends, made friendlier at the muzzle of a gun, James Beckworth III/ Mohammad ibn Mohammad al Islam and his compatriots had been led to this group in this dusty little hovel in Syria.

He had monitored the comings and goings of this group of ya Homaar associates until he was comfortable with their patterns. One simply couldn't barge in to a situation like this. One had to know one's enemy, know their patterns, and then put that knowledge to use. This is what gave him the advantage over the ya Homaar fools. This would be the day he would truly show Daesh his worth as a soldier.

• • •

In a crumbling three-story apartment building across the street from ya Homaar's Syrian hideout, catty-corner from the window from which Beckworth oiled his weapon, Avital Avraham, traveling under the name Amira Abramovitz, plopped her suitcase onto the foot of the full-sized bed, causing a plume of dust to erupt from the thin comforter. Unlike the way she had dressed in Jersey—flowing dresses with hair fashionably loose over her shoulders—she now wore some faded jeans and a white blouse tied off at the waist. Her hair was braided tightly to her head, and she glistened with sweat.

Remo, still traveling as Remo Robespierre, paced the room impatiently like a caged panther. He had traveled with a small duffel that carried only a change of khakis and a rolled up black t-shirt, which he had carelessly tossed into a chair too uncomfortable to be used for sitting.

"So which room are the Yahoo Martians holed up in?" he asked.

Avital wiped a bead of sweat from her forehead with the back of her hand, noticing that Remo didn't perspire in the slightest. Just another enigma about this CIA man she had stumbled into that she would worry about another day. Despite his seemingly nervous pacing, Avital saw that his breathing remained calm. It was the most self-possessed, controlled nervous pacing she had ever seen.

BULLY PULPIT

"They don't have one," she said.

He stopped. "They're not here? Then why are we?"

"They're not in this building," she emphasized. "They're in the building across the street. We're perfectly positioned to watch their comings and goings, establish their patterns of behavior and…"

The door clicked shut, and Avital realized she was alone. "Oh no," she said. "He wouldn't."

• • •

As James Beckworth III made a note about the last ya Homaar soldier to enter the building (making special attention to his rather effeminate gait), he looked up just in time to see a slender American in chinos stride purposefully across the street, in a straight line toward the ya Homaar safehouse. About fifty yards behind him, a woman in jeans rushed out of the building behind him, calling something out to him.

This stupid idiot was going to ruin everything—all his careful planning and waiting. Cursing, Beckworth grabbed his semi-automatic rifle and rushed out into the hallway, down the stairs, and out of the building, just in time to see the door to the ya Homaar hideout swing shut on a broken hinge.

• • •

The interior of the ya Homaar hole was a crumbling, dimly-lit room with half-broken furniture—more than half, now that Remo had crumpled one of the wooden support columns by means of an introduction.

"Okay, who wants to tell me where the bombs are coming from?" Remo asked, brushing the wood splinters from his palm. "I know none of you here are smart enough to build them. Tell me where to find your supplier, or I may get angry." The five men inside were agape at having seen this crazy American burst through their locked door and squeeze the supporting 4-by-4 like it was a toilet paper tube. One had the presence of mind to reach for the weapon on the table. Then his mind made its presence known in two gushing streams of blood and vitreous humour from the sockets his eyeballs had occupied just prior to Remo's fingers popping them.

"Bombs," Remo said again to the room of four statues. "El biggo kaboomo," he added, realizing the men in the room didn't understand plain English.

"*Qonbelah!*" Remo turned at the voice and saw Avital picking her way over the broken support beam. "*Qonbelah razzaq!*"

The men obviously understood her. Remo hooked a thumb in her direction. "What she said," he added, his eyes glinting menacingly from deep underneath his brow. Remo didn't understand the plaintive wailing, but got the hand gestures well enough to know they were pleading ignorance. Then he spied the backpack in the back of the room, set up against the corner. He pointed his chin at it. "You think there'll be a 'Property of' sticker anywhere in that?" he asked Avital.

She followed his gaze. "Only one way to find out," she

said. But as she moved toward the device, one of the men made a desperate lunge toward the table, slapping his hand on a boxlike remote, clearly intending to detonate the evidence, and all of them with it.

Nothing happened.

"Looks like you bought a dud, dead man," Remo said. His arm flicked out to the hand that held the remote, the fingertips brushing across the trapezium and powdering it against the scaphoid, rendering the man's thumb useless and infusing his forearm with an intense jolt of pain.

In the corner, hastened by panic at the attempted detonation, Avital had lifted the device out of the backpack and had slid a panel off the back of the device. "I wouldn't be too sure," she said. She tilted the device toward Remo so he could see the innards of the device, surrounding a small and unassuming digital display that was clearly active and counting down. The display showed three hours, twelve minutes, and seven seconds.

"Think you can disarm it in time?" Remo asked.

"Three hours might as well be forever," she said.

"Three hours is indeed plenty of time," said a voice from behind Remo. The voice was followed by a small click, and Remo felt the rushing pressure waves of the advancing bullet. He turned slightly, and the bullet passed harmlessly over his shoulder. Harmlessly to Remo, at least. It passed not so harmlessly through the forehead of the ya Homaar insurgent whose collar Remo was still gripping in one hand, snapping his neck back and spraying the floor behind him with flecks of red and gray.

"Finally, someone I can talk to," said Remo. He dropped the dead terrorist and seemed to materialize in front of the English speaking gunman, walking through two more bullets that could not have possibly missed at such range. The three remaining ya Homaar agents cowered behind a table, covering their eyes with their hands as Remo reached for the rifle. "Satan," one of them whispered as he observed an unharmed Remo disassemble the gun into unusable metal pieces of scrap.

James Beckworth III squeezed his finger on a trigger that suddenly wasn't there, before his knees were driven to the concrete floor. Remo's left hand squeezed his shoulder in a vise-like grip, sending screaming pain throughout his deltoid muscle. "Now what's a good American boy like you doing with a pond scum outfit like this?"

Grunting with pain, the young man tried to deliver a defiant "Death to America" as he had been trained, but a strangled cry was all he could manage until Remo let up the pressure on his nerve cluster.

"Never mind," Remo said. "Why don't you just tell me where you boys are getting these bombs? Because there's no way any of you are smart enough to be making them yourselves."

James Beckworth III gasped for breath. "I don't know," he whimpered, sounding much more now like an injured American child than an immortal freedom fighter. "I'm not with these wannabes. I'm Daesh!" He said the last bit with what he hoped sounded like pride. "I came to take their weapons, same as you."

Remo shook his head. "Not the same as me," he said, renewing his pressure on the nerve cluster and sending the man back to a dimension of blinding pain. "How you doing on defusing that thing, sweetheart?" he called back to Avital.

"Uhm, hello?" she said. She waggled her fingers in the air. "I can slide a panel off the side, but I didn't know I needed to bring a toolkit when you ran off to barge in blindly."

Remo nodded. "Fine, we'll bring it with us," he said. "Just give me a minute here to clean up." He pulled Beckworth in close by the collar of his shirt. "What did Daesh plan to use the bombs for?"

Beckworth stuck his chin out in defiance. Remo pushed it back in, erasing the investment Beckworth's parents had put into expensive orthodontics. "We're taking this bomb apart," Remo growled. "Talk, or we'll take you apart next." To emphasize his point, Remo's hand whipped past Beckworth's head, then dangled a bloody pale flap that Beckworth realized was his left ear. A searing pain enveloped the side of his head.

He talked. Remo listened, memorizing every detail of every plan to pass along to Smitty later.

"Okay, that's enough," Remo said. The ball of his right palm caught Beckworth across the left side of the forehead, denting it in like the shell of a hardboiled egg and sending bone fragments into his frontal lobe. His eyes rolled back into his head and he collapsed to the ground as Remo turned to the remaining ya Homaar with a tight, humorless grin.

As the dying men's screams escaped into the street, a returning ya Homaar insurgent saw the broken door frame and had the rare insight not to enter through it. He peeked through the window in time to see a slim white man dropping his brothers' lifeless bodies to the floor while a dark-haired woman was zipping up the backpack with their bomb in it. He backed away from the window and hurried down the street before taking out his phone and placing a call to report what he had witnessed.

• • •

The wilderness area was completely barren, and so remote that it took almost a week to reach civilization. There were buildings here, erected by men who came to study why the wilderness area was completely barren and who had ultimately decided that living a week away from the site was preferable to solving the mystery. The new occupants had surrounded the place with layers of electrified fencing, and hired a small army of Russian security officers to guard the place.

Less than ten miles from the outpost, Uri Kotov sat in a wooden shack that did little to keep the whistling wind from entering the shelter. His rifle sat propped up against one wall and he read the magazine he had with him for the fifteenth time. It never got old, perhaps because it was crowded with pictures of naked females in inviting poses.

Uri's partner, Boris Osin, reclined in his chair, snoring

loudly, giving Uri the freedom to enjoy his magazine in peace.

As Uri's mind concocted a scenario where he was entering the room to join with the platinum blonde with the large breasts who lay atop the polar bear rug, a new sound penetrated his fantasy—a high pitched, rapid beeping. Uri glanced at the device on the single desk the two men shared and saw the green light on it blinking. It had never blinked before, and never beeped. Uri slid the magazine back into the bottom drawer of the desk and nudged Boris awake.

"What do we do?" he asked.

Boris grunted. "Nothing yet," he replied. "We wait first."

The beeping and flashing synchronized and became more rapid until the light was a flicker and the sound was a constant sine wave. Then, a thousand yards outside their window, the small knapsack-sized bomb exploded in a fireball of light and fury.

When the rumbling subsided, Boris pulled himself out of his chair with another grunt. "I think we do something now," he said, shouldering his rifle.

"Do what? Where are you going?" Uri asked, standing to join his comrade.

"Is not difficult," Boris replied. "When bomb explodes, drive jeep to shed and get another one. Put new one where old one was. Do this before hour, hour and a half, go by." He shook his head. "Are small bombs. Seem useless," he mused.

"I remember the training," the younger man said

defensively. "It's just never happened before." He reached for his own rifle, planning to accompany his partner. Boris waved him back.

"Stay," he said. "Is small bomb. Is long drive. I go. You stay here with photo book of American whores." Uri blushed hotly, but Boris didn't seem to care as he stepped out into the freezing wind. Moments later, Uri heard the jeep crank over then drive off.

Uri re-opened the bottom drawer of the desk. He had at least an hour all to himself.

CHAPTER SIXTEEN

CHAIM SAID WAS LIVING A LIE. To anyone who knew him, he was a trusted agent of the Institute, a mechanical genius with an aptitude for technology. He'd been an asset to the Mossad on multiple occasions when it came to dismantling and deconstructing terrorist equipment. But if you could get Chaim to reveal his secrets, he would tell you that he was actually an American agent abroad, on the payroll of the Central Intelligence Agency, embedded with the Mossad to keep an eye on terrorist activity from an active and relatively friendly environment, even though Chaim knew the cardinal rule of being a spy: your friends are never your friends.

He awoke that morning to a strange chiming sound. After rifling through his drawer, he found the old beeper—an antique these days—displaying a number. He'd never heard it go off before, and was actually somewhat amazed that the batteries still worked.

He dialed the number it displayed. It rang twice and was answered with a terse, perfunctory order.

"A bomb has been recovered in Syria," the lemony sour voice on the other end said. "Examine it in detail and report back." Then the line went dead.

A short while later, Chaim's cell phone rang. This time he was expecting the call.

"Agent Said," the voice said. "We have an unexploded device taken from ya Homaar."

"We do?" Chaim replied, trying to sound surprised.

"Yes, but it's disarmed," the man on the other end replied. "One of our agents in the field defused it quite efficiently. Anyway, I've got orders to bring you in on the deconstruction team. The bosses want it gone over in detail to see if we can find anything about their suppliers."

"Right," Chaim replied. "Okay. Where do you need me to be?"

Within the hour, Chaim Said was on a transport to Safed, where a team of Mossad agents had smuggled the bomb across the Syrian border. In an underground room with white walls and glaring fluorescent lights, using needle-nose pliers, tweezers, and moveable magnification lenses, Said and three other men began the slow process of disassembling the bomb.

Said noted the internal timer. That had been of special note when the field agent had defused the bomb. Apparently whoever was supplying ya Homaar had their own agenda, and didn't trust the fledgling terror organization to know how to detonate the bombs properly. That, in and of itself, was curious, but not as curious as the otherwise relatively low-tech involved. The shielded copper wiring, the tightly-packed squares of C4...certainly it was a powerful explosion, but this was nowhere near the threat level of the suitcase nukes and dirty bombs that everyone always feared was coming.

Said was examining the shielding for any markings that might give away who engineered the bombs, when he caught sight of something just underneath the housing of the C4 components. Looking around quickly to make sure his teammates were occupied, he reached in with a pair of tweezers and pulled out a very tiny electronic object. "Hello there," Said murmured to himself. "What's a nice little device like you doing in a bomb like this?"

• • •

"A transmitter?" The bitter, pinched voice that answered Said's call sounded unimpressed. "A hidden timer inside the casing, and a secondary backup in case that fails."

"No sir," Chaim said. "You're thinking of a receiver. This device is made to *send out* a signal, not receive one. It's very delicate," he added.

"I know exactly what a transmitter does," came the terse response. "Can you determine what it was transmitting?"

"No sir, but I can tell you on which frequency." Chaim rattled off a series of numbers. "There was something else odd about it," he added.

"More odd than what you've already discovered?"

"Yes sir," he said. "From what I can tell—and I must be wrong—the thing was wired to send out a signal just moments after the detonation of the bomb. That seems like bad timing, if you ask me. I mean, the explosion would have vaporized this thing, so it wouldn't send out any signal at all."

"Assuming the bomb detonated," the voice said plainly.

Said opened his mouth to respond, but got cut off.

"Thank you, Agent Said," the voice said before closing the connection.

• • •

The noise of the constant vehicle and foot traffic never subsided outside the unassuming *gassho* style house in Kawagoe City. The doors were customized to be a foot wider than standard. The bathtub was extra-large, the kitchen sported two restaurant style double-door refrigerators, and the toilets were industrial strength stainless steel.

A telephone rang, and somehow through the cacophony of passing music, honking horns, people shouting, cars backfiring, and the occasional gunshot, the jangling was heard. An elephantine arm the girth of a tree limb reached for the receiver.

"Moshi moshi." The greeting rumbled through prodigious lips that smacked when they formed words. Jowls jiggled from the simplest of mandibular activity.

"Mushy yourself, Big Asshole," the flirty female voice responded from the other end.

Asashoryu Hakuho, aka The Big As Ho, smiled. "This is a funny call," he said. "Only two women could call me that, and they are both dead."

"Aw, he remembers us," came a second female voice,

fainter, indicating she was further away from the phone.

Big As Ho smiled wider, revealing an expansive set of teeth which still had bits of lunch, breakfast, and last night's dinner wedged into the crevices. "Ladies," he exclaimed. "How may I be of service to you?"

"We just have a teensy little favor to ask of you, big guy," the voice purred.

"For you, I would kill a man," he joked.

Musical laughter tittered across the line. "It's so funny you should put it that way," she said.

• • •

Remo sat with his elbows on his knees, his chin resting in both hands. His unpacked bag sat tossed in the corner where he had absently and expertly tossed it upon arrival back at his set of suites at La Haule Manor. He had left Avital downstairs without saying a word, which seemed to be fine with her as she hadn't spoken to him the entire trip back. Apparently she had only come because he had rushed them both out so quickly that she had left most of her personal belongings behind.

Chiun lay prone on the wheeled hospital bed, looking more and more like a model of a man made out of vellum parchment draped around a skeleton of Popsicle sticks. Remo thought about how much death the two of them had seen together, how inured they had both become to it. Remo even know that, if given the orders from Upstairs, he would kill Chiun or Chiun would kill him. But this was different. If he had to kill Chiun, Chiun would understand—that was the business. He would even respect Remo for it. This was someone else killing him—hell, the accidental byproduct, really, even though the killer's intent was one of global genocide. That ought to have made it the most impersonal of killings, but Remo was taking it very personally.

Remo felt the displacement of air in the room indicating that someone had joined the doctor and the two nurses who were perpetually on duty to see to the comatose Korean. The attending scent of jasmine wasn't necessary for Remo to know Avital had come in. She pulled up a chair next to him beside Chiun's bed and sat in silence with him for several minutes.

"So are you never going to speak to me again?" she asked. "Not even to say goodbye?"

Remo looked at her as if she had asked him why purple giraffes were singing the multiplication tables. "Not talking to you? I thought you weren't talking to me?"

"Well, I was upset for a while with you," she admitted with a shrug. "What with the way you rushed in headlong without a plan..."

"I had a plan."

"Oh, you had a plan?"

"Yep," he said. "Go in and start killing until someone gave us answers about the bomb, then kill the rest of them."

"That was your plan?"

"Did I kill them?"

"Yes."

"Do you have the bomb?"

"Yes."

"Then I had a plan."

Avital sighed. "We still don't know who's supplying their ordnance," she said.

Remo couldn't tell her that the man she was looking for was the esteemed Reverend Billy Walker, for the same reasons he couldn't tell her why the reverend was supplying the bombs. If anyone else found out it was Walker, they might also learn about the processes he was employing. "We'll find who they are," he said. "I'm sure your team will find some clue."

"You understand I had to turn the bomb over to my colleagues," she said. "I couldn't just give it over to the CIA."

Remo tilted his head at her. "You thought I was worried about that?" he asked. "I'm not. I want to get to the son of a bitch behind this as much as you do. Probably more. It doesn't matter to me which outfit points me in his direction."

"And then what?" she asked. "You'll rush in and kill whomever it is?"

He gave her a lopsided, humorless grin. "That's the biz, sweetheart."

She sighed. "You're a much colder man than I could have imagined," she said. And then she was silent again.

Five minutes later, she held his hand in hers, and they listened to the steady beep-beep-beep of the heart monitor deep into the night.

CHAPTER SEVENTEEN

THE PLANE'S MOTORS STRAINED under the weight of the cargo, putting unwitting populations at risk with each town the plane passed over.

The jet had but one passenger, and the stewardess (who had become resigned to the fact that the passenger was never going to use the phrase "flight attendant") was wheeling the catering cart for the third time from the galley in the back. She had wondered why such a large quantity of food was being loaded before takeoff, especially for a chartered flight carrying just one man. Now she wondered if they had packed enough, and whether the tires would survive the impact with the tarmac when the pilot and co-pilot finally brought them in for a landing. She knew one thing for certain—she wasn't going to be anywhere nearby when they were looking for someone to clean the restroom.

The mid-seat armrests had been removed, opening up the row of three seats for the girth of Asashoryu Hakuho. A paper bucket sat in the aisle, overflowing with the shiny calcium carcasses of chickens who had given their lives for the benefit of The Big As Ho. "Stewardess!" he grumbled in a deep baritone that shook through the plane like turbulence.

The pert little blonde sighed. *Chin up, shoulders back, tits out*, she thought to herself as she pushed the cart up beside The Big As Ho, nudging the chicken bucket away with the tip of her flats.

"More chicken, Mr. Hakuho?" she asked. She hoped not, as the rotisserie was now an empty cage of grease droppings.

"When do we land?" he growled. He untied the garbage-bag sized bib that protected his shirt from dribbles. Nothing protected his chins, however, so he used a fistful of wet napkins to push crumbs from the furrowed expanse of rubbery flesh that ran from his lower lip to his collarbone.

Not soon enough, she thought. As if in answer to her silent prayer, a chime sounded and the pilot's voice came through the speakers. "We're about 90 kilometers out from Jersey Airport, and should be touching down in about 20 minutes. We hope you've enjoyed your flight and will keep us in mind the next time you need air travel."

The stewardess rolled her eyes. *Frank's laying it on a bit thick for a single passenger*, she thought. *Then again, he gets the lion's share of the money, so why shouldn't he?*

The Big As Ho smiled to himself. "Just enough time for dessert," he rumbled. "Bring the pies," he said.

"Right away, sir," she said, with her best plastic smile. The pies were stored in a rolling pie safe in the galley. "Do you want the apple, cherry or coconut crème?"

The Big As Ho turned toward her, his cheeks all but obscuring his eyes.

"Yes," he said with complete sincerity, and he licked his lips in anticipation.

• • •

Remo could have ordered in. He could probably have asked Avital. Hell, a call to Smitty, and he could have had a personal chef sent to the room. But much as he didn't want to leave Chiun's side, he also needed the air, to stretch his legs—to breathe.

He purposefully took a route that avoided pedestrian traffic. With every passing hour, he could feel his center slipping. He paused beneath a tree, and inhaled, inhaled until his lungs were stretched to capacity, and held it. Then he released it, all at once, with a scream that was as much a part of his basic Sinanju training as it was a much needed release of frustration.

Almost instantly, he felt more centered—so much so that he was surprised at how off-centered he had become. He noticed his skin was more sensitive to the air currents. He noticed the sound of the leaves brushing against each other at the top of the tree.

He noticed the SUV.

• • •

The SUV had the rear seats removed to make room for The Big As Ho. The girls had told him that his target had been followed to a charter plane in Syria, and that this plane had filed a flight plan to Jersey. They had described the man with the skinny body and the thick wrists, but it was The Big As Ho who figured out a man of such power would demand a place that bespoke such power. The driver of the SUV had grown impatient, but was too afraid to leave the car after his first attempt had earned him a crushed shoulder from a beefy paw. Fortunately he had the extra-large cup that had begun its day full of coffee, and which having been emptied was now approaching being full of kidney-filtered coffee.

When the skinny man with the thick wrists stepped out the front of La Haule Manor, it was with a mixture of dread and relief that the driver obeyed the grumbled order to follow him, slowly and at a distance. The vehicle shook, and the driver wondered if they were experiencing aftershocks from the recent earthquake that still had everyone talking. When he checked his rearview mirror, he saw that the shaking was caused by his passenger, who was chuckling giddily as he watched the man in the khaki slacks wander off into the open park away from the road.

The walking man then stopped and seemed to sag, then released a roar into the sky. They're both crazy, the driver decided.

"Park here," The Big As Ho growled, when the thin man turned and looked directly at the SUV. "I will only be moments."

"Yes, sir," the driver lied.

• • •

If Chiun weren't nearly dead, this would kill him, Remo scolded himself when he realized just how out of tune he had become. He had foolishly thought that the only symptom he was experiencing from the global quakes was the persistent waves of nausea—and, of course, there was the impending coma he had to look forward to. The other symptoms had been so subtle he had not even noticed them. Now that he knew about them, he couldn't help but be keenly aware of how muffled they were getting.

He could feel the gazes coming at him from the SUV just long enough to be alerted to its presence. Now that he stared back at it, he saw the passenger door slide open. The SUV disgorged a gelatinous mass of flesh and black silk. Once the opening was cleared, the SUV took off with a squeal of its tires, the passenger door sliding almost shut from the inertia.

The blob of flesh stood and took on a form something like a man. The face appeared pinched and tiny on the blob that passed for a head, but Remo realized it was a regular sized face—it was the head that was fat.

The face grinned as the shoulders sloughed off the black silk kimono, showing off the rolls and rolls of flesh. Only a shimmering black mawashi kept the figure on the legal side of decency.

A thick beefy arm raised and pointed directly at Remo. Somewhere a storm must have been coming in, because a sound like thunder rolled across the park, sounding an awful lot like "You!"

"About time somebody sent somebody after me," Remo said. "I was starting to feel unappreciated. Care to tell me where your check comes from? I probably already know who signed it, but knowing where they are would really save me a lot of time."

BULLY PULPIT

The Big As Ho assumed his attack stance, coming at Remo. He stomped once. Then he stomped with the other leg.

And, because the gods have a sense of humor, when he stomped the third time, the ground shook across the entirety of the island. In the distance, Remo could hear people screaming and things crashing, as the P-waves washed over his body, bringing renewed disorientation and nausea. Somewhere somebody was laughing, and Remo realized the sound was coming from the nearly-naked giant who had somehow appeared right next to him.

Two fleshy arms with the girth of tree trunks and the consistency of bags of pancake batter wrapped themselves around his shoulders, crushing in on him with an elephantine weight. Remo made quick strikes with the fingertips of both hands where he hoped the man's kidneys were. He broke the skin and sank his fingers into the knuckles.

The man only laughed harder and squeezed tighter. Remo wanted to vomit—partly because he thought about all the human grease that now coated his fingers. His vision blackened around the edges until all he could see was the leering face of the human python. His range of motion was limited, and every nerve cluster he considered striking, he realized, was buried under so much insulation that they were almost impossible to reach. Nearly all of the man was padded.

Nearly all, Remo realized. He drew his neck back and struck with his forehead hard against the bridge of the walking whale's nose. He felt the satisfying crackle like popping a wad of bubble wrap, and felt a rush of wetness against his face. As he dropped to the ground, he rolled on impact and rose to his feet in a single smooth action.

Free from the crushing grip and able to breathe once more, Remo now had infinite opportunities to finish his opponent quickly. Quickly, however, wasn't the way Remo wanted this to go. Someone had obviously sent this guy after him, which meant he had to be getting close to Walker, and this guy was going to tell Remo everything he needed to know to find him.

The man-mountain reached blindly for Remo, blood from his nose painting his face and stinging his eyes. Since that seemed to irritate him, Remo's arm flashed out and his fingernails grazed the brute's forehead. A thin red line appeared and began to weep redness down over his eyebrows.

"Come on, sweetheart," said Remo. "Tell me where the preacher is while you can still talk."

In reply, The Big As Ho lunged for Remo, flailing blindly. Remo sidestepped him easily, but in the fat man's current state almost anyone could avoid him. Remo tripped him just for fun, then wished he hadn't as the impact with the gravel path through the greenspace caused his mawashi to slip and expose his gelatinous glutes.

Remo stood by patiently as The Big As Ho pushed himself back to his feet. "Enough!" he roared. "Now you will face the power of The Big As Ho!"

Remo rolled his eyes. It was always the worst when they

named themselves. "Normally, I could go on like this all day, lardass, but I'm on a bit of a deadline," Remo said. He glanced around, and his eyes fell on the knee-high posts that lined the walkway. They were each tipped with solar lamps so that the path would be lit in the evenings. "So are you going to tell me where the reverend is or not?"

The Big As Ho shook as he chuckled. "Why do you continue to ask for a holy man? Is it because you know you are going to die?"

Remo sighed. "Let's see if I can jog your memory," he said. He stepped in close to The Big As Ho, slipping his leg behind one ankle, ducking his head out of the range of the groping arms, and pushing against his alternate shoulder.

The Big As Ho was swiveled about, and brought to a crunching seated position. His eyes grew wide and blood trickled from the corner of his mouth.

Having a two-foot post shoved up his backside gave The Big As Ho an amazing amount of total recall. Remo took advantage of this situation with a quick interrogation and learned:

"I don't know about any reverend. Please help me."

"It was the women. I think I'm dying."

"They wired the money to my account. I think I'm going to be sick."

"They did not say where they were. Oh God."

"Exact words? One said 'Goodbye.' The other said '*Do svidaniya*' and laughed, and the first one told her to shut up. I need a doctor."

When Remo knew he wasn't going to get any more information, he put his hand on The Big As Ho's shoulder and pulled him forward, stepping back and walking away as he did. The results of the angular extraction left The Big As Ho with what the attending medical examiner would write down in his autopsy notes as "the worst case of rectal prolapse in known history."

CHAPTER EIGHTEEN

FOR A MAN ON ONE OF THE MOST restrictive diets on Earth, Remo was always surprised at how often he found himself eating crow. Of course, it was usually served by Chiun and he didn't have a choice. Serving it to himself and involving Smitty was one of the least enjoyable things in his life.

"Your preacher is off the hook," Remo said when the phone was answered.

Doctor Harold W. Smith was taken aback only slightly, but his sour disposition wasn't capable of taking any enjoyment in Remo's discomfort. "On the contrary," he replied, "I'm afraid he is very much 'on the hook.'"

"Smitty, I just went a rather ugly round with the offspring of Sasquatch and the Pillsbury Doughboy, and the intel he gave me points to somebody else. Two female 'somebody elses' in fact," he added.

"Where did you come across this information?" Smith asked.

"Some big asshole," Remo said. "Tried to do the business on me. Damn near succeeded, too, by the way, and thanks for your concern. Whatever whammy these earthquakes put on Chiun, it's starting to affect me as well. And right now the best we can hope for is to continue to put a kink in their schedule."

"So your plan is to find a different bomb every one hour and forty-nine minutes and stop it from detonating?" Smith asked flatly. "You're fast, but you're nowhere near that fast. Besides, it's not working."

Smith explained how the recovered bomb had revealed a hidden transmitter, one that triggered only milliseconds after the detonation timer hit zero.

"So basically what you're saying is that someone's getting notice if a bomb doesn't go off..." Remo said, his voice trailing off.

"That they probably have a backup bomb that goes off somewhere else," Smith replied.

"So that's that, then," Remo said. "It's been a fun ride, Smitty, but I'm going to go cram a fulfilling life into the last few days I have left."

"There is an upside to knowing this," Smith said.

"You know how I live for your nuggets of optimism," Remo replied.

"To be prepared to set off a backup bomb on a moment's notice," Smith said calmly, "they would need to have a stationary base of operations. Some place where they could stockpile their explosives and have a fresh one ready in less than two hours."

"Find their base, find their bombs," Remo said. "Seems

simple enough. Oh, but wait, it's still a pretty big planet, isn't it?"

"Did your assailant mention anything at all that might hint as to a location?" Smith asked.

Remo considered. "He said it was two girls," he said. "They seemed pretty flirty to be hiring a killer. And one might be Russian."

"Russian?" Smith said. Over the phone Remo could hear keys tapping as Smith worked his computer console.

"Just a guess," Remo said. "He said one of them gave him a Russian goodbye."

"I don't see anyone with close ties to Russia working in Walker's main headquarters," Smith said, scanning once more the list of employees that constantly yielded him no solid results.

"Smitty, I'm telling you, the Walker thing's a red herring."

"But I did get a trace on the black box of Walker's private jet," Smith continued undeterred. "It went off the radar after entering Russian air space."

"Wait a second," Remo said. "So your theory is a guy who has apparently gone to Russia, and my source pins it to two girls who might be in Russia. I don't know. That's still pretty iffy."

"Here's something that's not," Smith said tersely. "A number of Russian male citizens, all former military, have applied for jobs as security personnel for a special project."

"I don't suppose this special project has a name?"

"No. And all the men have disappeared. Some of their family have filed complaints that they've gone missing."

"But they're not missing," Remo said. "They're just hidden somewhere. Maybe guarding a big old pile of bombs?"

"That's an assumption," Smith said. "But it's all we have to go on."

"Two girls, a bunch of Russian soldiers, and a preacher," Remo said. "Sounds like a party."

"None of the men said where they were going, but I've been able to trace the paths of more than a few of them based on incidental transactions made after they applied for the positions, and were presumably hired," said Smith. "Of those, nearly eighty percent of them all seem to be converging on a remote village of Vanavara. It's something of a tourist town."

"Vanavara?" Remo said. "That's pretty far north. Be pretty cold this time of year for Russian sightseeing."

More taps. "It's not that kind of tourism," Smith said. "Vanavara is just the origin point for expeditions to the real attraction. That's where Walker's base will be."

"I'll bite," Remo said. "Where is that?"

Smith sighed. It was too perfect, both from a tactical sense as well as a philosophical one, not to be accurate. It was where the meteorite didn't hit, where Tesla's experiment may or may not have caused a hole in the Earth.

"Tunguska."

• • •

The Reverend Billy Walker was uncomfortable

wandering the grey, shadowed hallways of the greater concrete structure. His quarters, if he didn't open the door, looked on the inside to be at least a close facsimile to his office back in California, betrayed only by the washed out quality of the sunlight that filtered through the casement windows near the top of his wall.

He'd been to Russia before, of course. He'd had a couple of televised revivals here, once Glasnost set in and the country opened its borders and its minds. But he'd always gone where there were people, where there were hearts to be won and souls to be saved.

There wasn't a soul to be found in Tunguska, except for those that had been hired on to provide security and cycle the ordnance when needed — and their souls, much like his, were beyond saving.

He paused before the door that was his destination and knocked twice.

"Come in," a youthful voice replied on the other side. The Reverend Walker cast his eyes downward and opened the door. The last time he had walked in, invited, he inadvertently caught a glimpse of the girls in just their skivvies. He hadn't meant to see what he saw, and apologized profusely for the intrusion while blushing hotly. He didn't want to repeat that incident, and was glad that the girls had not taken affront to his accidental invasion of their privacy.

"We're decent," one of the girls said with a giggle. He looked up and blushed anyway. Yes, they were covered —

literally covered—with a sheet up to their necks as they lay side by side in the double bed. Under the sheet, however, it was clear to him that the sisters were naked.

"Did I wake you?" he asked, tremulously.

They smiled. "Who could sleep through the sound of that blast?" the one on the left teased.

"Yes. Right," he said. "That's actually what I came to talk to you about. Was that the backup plan, or did something go wrong?"

The one on the right sat up, propped against a pillow, holding the sheet to her breasts with one hand, her bare shoulders revealed. "Both," she said. "That was the backup plan, and something did go wrong."

"Oh?" Walker stammered.

"Nothing to be worried about," the girl on the left assured him. She sat up as well now, and leaned in close to the other, sharing the cover the sheet afforded. But it was such a sheer sheet, and it clung to them the way only silk can, revealing contours and curves, the swells of their breasts, capped off with a clearly delineated and pert nipple. Despite the cold, the Reverend Walker could feel a trickle of sweat trail down his left temple. He knew he had to be blushing, because the girls began to giggle. They always took such innocent childlike delight in the embarrassment of an old man. "One of the bombs that was supposed to go off...Well, it didn't," she continued. "So, we set off one of the backups. Just as we planned."

He wiped the bead of sweat from his cheek. "Will it..."

he began. "I mean, is there a chance that we might have to do it again?"

The girl on the right shrugged, raising those bare shoulders and pushing her breasts further against the sheet with the noncommittal motion. With the drop of her shoulders, her breasts continued moving for a second longer. "Hard to say," she said. "We've taken steps that ought to take care of the matter, but you just never know."

"I understand," Walker said. "It's just that, well, as you explained to me earlier, I thought we couldn't achieve the goal if we set them all off at the same location. We had to, you know, spread them out."

They smiled, so sweetly, as if they knew so much and put up with him knowing so little. "Yes, that's right, Billy," said the girl sitting up against the left pillow. "But that was only in the beginning."

"By now, things are so far in motion that we can afford more than a couple of double taps on the same spot," the other added.

"So we're that far along?" he asked hopefully. "The goal is in sight?"

"Another day or two," she replied, "and not even God himself could stop what we've got going."

He silently asked God to forgive them the blasphemy cloaked in their confident statement, but he knew God wasn't listening to his prayers any longer.

"Good," he said. "That's very good."

The first girl patted a narrow spot between her and the

other girl on the bed. "Want to spend the last days in paradise?" she cooed. "Always room for one more."

He chuckled and looked at the floor once more. "Girls, one of these days, I'm going to more than half-think you're serious."

"Not many of those days left to think that," she said.

"No," he said, shuffling toward the door. "Not many of those days left at all."

CHAPTER NINETEEN

REMO, HIS BAG PACKED, OPENED the door of his suite to a raised female fist. His hand instinctively shot up, and he just as quickly countermanded his instinct and brought it down.

Avital blinked. "Do you always answer the door ready for a fight?" she asked.

"We have a lot of Jehovah's Witnesses in my neighborhood," he said. "Look, I was just getting ready to go out, so I can't stay and chat."

"Go out?" she asked, glancing at his duffel. "Looks like you're on more than just an errand."

"Actually, it is just an errand," Remo said. "A few errands." She shook her head. "Okay, they're not exactly local errands."

"I'm still packed, and I'm coming with you," she said, pushing past him.

"Really, I don't have time for you to run back to your room and get your things."

She picked up a small valise sitting in the corner of the room. "Ready to go," she said. She gave him a coy smile. "Actually, I was coming down to retrieve this anyway. I left it here earlier."

Remo was about to argue when the phone chirped.

"Your transport is ready," Harold Smith informed him through the phone.

"Aunt Mildred," Remo replied. "Now's not really a good time."

"She's there?" Smith asked. "Does she know about the bombs?"

"No, no, Aunt Mildred, nothing like that."

"Large family you have there," Avital whispered.

"Remo, I need not remind you that anyone who learns about Walker's plan…"

"Yes, I understand, Aunt Mildred," Remo said. "Uncle Fred's drinking won't be a problem, I'm sure. You take care. My love to Aunt Brunhilde."

Avital raised an eyebrow, and Remo shrugged. He tucked the phone back into his pants pocket.

"Okay," he said. "If you're coming with me, then we have to scoot." He ushered her out the door and allowed himself one brief glimpse at Chiun's hospital bed, and listened until he'd heard three steady beeps from the heart monitor. They were coming further apart. "Be back soon, Little Father," he whispered.

• • •

It didn't feel so long ago that a mission into Russia would have involved a C-141 Starlifter, a B-1 stealth plane, and a HALO jump. But these were more civilized times. Now, a flight into Russia was just a matter of buying a ticket. His first class ticket was waiting for him, and by the time they arrived at the airport, one would be waiting for Avital as well.

"I don't know what you're following me for," Remo said quite innocently on the taxi ride to the airport after Avital had hung up with some whiny fellow named Ephraim. "You've already recovered...equipment," he said.

"But we don't know who manufactured the...equipment," she said, cutting her eyes at the taxi driver and maintaining Remo's subtlety of conversation. "And I'm willing to bet that you do know."

"Me?" Remo replied. "I'm just out for a much needed change of scenery."

"Of course you are," Avital said. She leaned back against the back seat of the cab. "As am I. And we both know how beautiful northern Russia is in the wintertime." She snuggled up next to Remo as though already feeling the cold. "I've always wanted to experience an American Christmas."

"I thought you were Jewish?"

"Presents are presents," she said with a girlish smile. "One can never get too many of those, regardless of the reason."

"What happened to 'better to give than to receive?'"

"Spoken like someone who has never received," she said confidently. Remo smiled. She so reminded him of Chiun at times. No wonder he liked her.

"I'm not completely without charity," she said with a pout, before turning serious. "I just don't know where to send my money." She sighed. "I want to help the earthquake victims, but..." She held her arms out. "But which ones? They're everywhere it seems. Something really, really strange is going on, and if I wasn't so focused on ya Homaar..." Her voice trailed off. For the first time, she looked meek and helpless.

Remo knew exactly how she felt, but more strongly, because he knew exactly what was causing the earthquakes, and it ate at his gut. He looked out the window at the passing traffic. By his reckoning, sometime in the last five minutes another bomb had gone off somewhere in the world, and at least five more would have detonated before he would make it all the way to Vanavara, at which point he was going to have to come up with a method of shaking Avital off his tail. But for now, he kept his arm around her and pulled her close. With Chiun's life hanging by a thread, and the world literally in the balance, he allowed himself the luxury of human contact for the duration of the trip.

• • •

One taxi, one plane ride, and one helicopter lift later, and the remote outpost town of Vanavara had two more people walking its desolate streets. Remo helped Avital down from the chopper, then quietly tipped the pilot five hundred American dollars and whispered something to him. The pilot pocketed the five bills and nodded before taking off.

"Doesn't he need to refuel or something?" Avital shouted over the roar of the rotors.

Remo shrugged. "I'm not the pilot."

Avital looked around. "So, we're here," she said, pulling her down coat tightly around her to brace against the whipping wind. She had no idea how Remo could stand it in just a long sleeved white turtleneck and matching chinos. "Final destination, you said. So, which of these guys is our bomb builder?"

"Patience, grasshopper," Remo said, guiding her by the elbow away from the landing pad and toward a row of shops. "Vanavara is actually something of a tourist stop—albeit for a rather crazy breed of tourist. Let's catch our breath and then we'll lay out a plan."

In the first shop they entered, Remo found what he was looking for. Vodka. He had a feeling he could find the same bottle in any of the half-dozen shops in town.

"Really?" she asked, as he pocketed the bottle and walked down the main (and apparently only) street into the heart of Vanavara.

"All part of the plan," he said. "We need to blend in and look like we belong." As they got further down the street, he pulled the bottle back out and unscrewed the cap. "Here, you need to take a swig." To demonstrate, he tilted the bottle back and drained some into his mouth.

Avital was unsure of what Remo's plan was, but she knew two things for certain. One, he was the craziest American she'd ever encountered. Two, he was always right. She took the bottle and took one hesitant swallow of the burning liquid, as she felt Remo's hand on her shoulder steadying her. Then her knees went out from under her and everything went dark.

As Avital crumpled, Remo caught her with one arm. He then proceeded to spray out the vodka he'd been holding in his cheek, spitting it all over the street. He poured a little bit more vodka over the front of Avital's coat and tossed the remainder of the bottle into a corner trash can.

He kept one arm under Avital, and held one of her arms around his shoulders. To anyone looking on, it would appear as if he were helping an incredibly drunk girlfriend home. And when Remo was certain that nobody was looking, he deposited Avital's unconscious form on a bench outside a building marked 'POLITSIYA' and quickly strolled away. Within moments he knew an officer would find her and take her in for public drunkenness. And if the officer did anything more than put her in a holding cell overnight, he'd deal with that when he returned.

If he returned.

He could hear the approach of the helicopter as he neared their original landing site, and when it touched down he lightly hopped up into the front seat beside the pilot.

"Don't you need to refuel or something?" Remo asked loudly over the roar of the blades. The pilot grinned and shrugged, and Remo decided he was better off not knowing.

• • •

The copter flew north north-east, over miles of snow covered desolation. There was no human life out here, none that had any sense anyway. Remo had instructed the pilot to let him down about five miles to the south of his destination—the Tunguska archeological site, which now lay largely abandoned. Remo hadn't been lying when he told Avital that Vanavara was a tourist site; it was where anyone wanting to tour the big hole in the ground that was Tunguska would set off with a tour guide, and then spend the next nine days over rough terrain before taking selfies with a bunch of nothing behind them.

The tours did not run in the winter, which was the bulk of the year, because the terrain was impassable with deep snow.

A few miles short of the drop point, the copter banked to the left.

"Hey," Remo shouted. Then louder, "Hey!" He pointed to the ground. "We're not there yet," he shouted over the roar of the blades.

The pilot shrugged and grinned sheepishly. To emphasize his point, he tapped on the glass cover of the fuel gauge. "Refuel," he said in a thick Russian accent. "Turn now."

Remo rolled his eyes. "Hey, look! Is that the Abominable Snowman?" He pointed past the pilot to his left. As the pilot's gaze followed, Remo undid his harness and let himself fall backward from the copter. It was only a few hundred feet—granted, he was expecting the copter to go in lower, or at least get near snow level when he was ready to disembark, but it was a workable exit. What pissed him off the most as he picked his landing spot and went into guided freefall was that he was going to have to hike about three more miles than he had expected over snow. It wouldn't affect him so much, but it was the extra time — time he and the planet didn't have to spare.

He straightened his body and neatly dove at an angle into a snowdrift several feet deep, swimming through the stuff like the water that it was and emerging several yards away.

"There goes your tip," Remo muttered at the vanishing copter, then turned away from it and oriented his body in the direction of the facility. "Could have at least dropped me off on the other side of those hills," he groused as he began running. With each step, his footfalls climbed higher into the snow, until within the space of a football field he was skimming along the top of it.

He was about halfway up the hill when the tremor struck. Remo had about two seconds of warning, for all the good it gave him, as he felt the advancing P-waves send a wave of nausea through his intestines.

The hill felt it, too, and sent a wave of something else — a cascading tsunami of snow that crashed into him, sweeping him downward and burying him under so many feet of whiteness that all became black.

• • •

The first thing Remo noticed was that he was breathing rapidly and shallowly. Most people would feel panic in such a scenario, but curiously Remo's first emotion was embarrassment. Sinanju was breathing, and if he couldn't even do that correctly, he didn't deserve to breathe at all. He would fail the planet, but worse than that, he would fail Chiun.

Getting control of his breathing, however, proved to be more difficult than he expected. There was very little in the way of air around his body, and he had no way of knowing which way was up.

"*Breathe.*"

"Easy for you to say, Little Father," Remo said to the voice in his head. "You've got hoses feeding you all the oxygen you can handle."

"*Breathe!*"

Remo strove for a deep breath, and aspirated a mouthful of ice crystals. He coughed. "There's not enough air," he muttered weakly.

"*Complaints,*" the voice in his head chided him. "*Always you complain. 'The ground is too hard.' 'I want a hamburger.' Why I was left to train such a weak, pale piece of a pig's ear, the gods only know.*"

"Shut the hell up and let me die in peace," Remo grumbled.

"*What is snow?*" Chiun's voice intoned. "*What is snow but water? What is water? What is water but oxygen and less than oxygen? All around you, there is oxygen. Breathe!*"

Bringing his hands up to his face in the darkness, Remo cupped them over his mouth. Then he opened them, and let his palms fill with snow, scraping it from the wall pressing in on him. His hands filled, he rubbed his palms together, melting the snow into water, then evaporating the water into steam. He took a breath and did this again, then again.

When he had hollowed out sufficient space, he took a pinch of snow in one hand and held his other hand beside it. He let it go. The snow went sideways, hitting him in the face. Up was straight ahead of him.

Burrowing, taking few breaks to melt more snow into a breath of air, Remo made his way arduously toward what had to be the surface. The blackness gradually turned into gray, then white, and he broke through into sweet, thin air, filling his lungs. Centering himself, he found he was once again at the foot of the hills.

Remo shook himself. "Once more unto the breach," he said aloud. He began marching up the side of the snow-covered hills, this time letting his legs sink into the snow, happy to be alive, and ready to deliver death.

CHAPTER TWENTY

REMO ARRIVED AT THE OUTSKIRTS of a facility surrounded by chain link and armed guards. Topping the chain link was razor wire, its lack of tarnish providing evidence that it was recently added. The snow landing on him did not melt, as Remo concentrated on keeping his surface temperature even with that of the air. After several minutes, the snowflakes had caked around his body, effectively camouflaging him against the whiteness of the surrounding landscape.

As he surveyed the layout of the compound and the position of the guards, an explosion to the west sent shockwaves through the ground and, Remo knew, into it as well. He muttered a curse that Mother Earth had gotten one more kick in the crotch because he hadn't arrived sooner. No more, he decided. This had to end now, or everything else was going to end soon.

Remo ran silently atop the snow. His feet left no impression, and his breath emitted no steam. He approached the pair of guards at what he presumed was the main gate. He had one hour and forty-nine minutes before another blast would go off, and with Smitty tying up all the construction and mining projects in a sea of red tape, the odds were with him that the next explosion was going to be right here.

The guards conversed in their native Russian, sharing tales of how they were going to spend the exorbitant salaries they were being paid when they got back to civilization—where they could get such civilized things as hookers and vodka. It gave Remo a warm feeling that capitalism and western values had gained such a foothold in Russia—almost as warm as the feeling he got seeing the priceless expression on the guard's face when he saw his partner's head slump sideways onto his shoulder and lay there before rolling to his chest, attached to his body by nothing more than the skin of his neck. Remo's snow-camouflaged body gave him an extra degree of invisibility on top of that already granted him through his Sinanju skills. The guard, assuming the attack had come from a shot in the distance, raised his rifle and aimed it in one direction, then another, desperately trying to focus on a target, any target. By that time, Remo had already gotten behind him. The Kalashnikov disappeared from his hands, and hit the ground in pieces. The guard gaped at the useless metal fragments, then his eyes rolled back as a tap to the base of his neck turned off the power to his brain.

The guards dispatched, Remo fingers flew over the chain link of the fence, disassembling the joints like a series of simple Chinese puzzles, unzipping the metal barrier until there was a hole large enough to slip through. But once inside the compound, Remo was confronted with a secondary fence—this one unguarded, but electrified. Remo could feel the hum of it as he approached, shaking his head that people still found something so fatally flawed to be a deterrent to entry. The technology was originally designed to contain cattle, and most people were not much smarter than that anyway. Remo shook his head in disgust at the lack of a challenge. He reached for the live feeder wire, feeling the current dance across his skin. He gave a short hop, both his feet leaving the ground before snapping the wire between his thumb and forefinger, severing both the wire and the flow of current while not being grounded himself; then he stepped between the barbed wires and made his way further inward.

"I could really use a mall directory right about now," he muttered. Most of the buildings looked the same: mottled gray cubes with one gray door and no windows. "Smitty would love this. He could summer here and get away from all that dreadful color."

Another guard stepped out of one of the doors Remo was passing. The door closed, and the guard would never go back in again.

Fifteen minutes had passed already, as Remo kept track in his mind, counting heartbeats to supplement what used to be an autonomic ability. At every turn he found another armed security guard to dispatch. Finally, he turned a corner and found a larger building near the center of the compound. It was wide enough to hold several semis, with a second floor for offices. More telling, it had windows, and some lights were on.

"Honey, I'm home," he announced as he shouldered into the door.

Inside, he found five more guards, seated around a folding table playing poker, using potato as chips.

The first one to stand was the first one to die, as the outside edge of Remo's hand made an upward sweep against the bridge of his nose, sending splinters of bone and cartilage up into the guard's frontal lobe. A second dumped the table over, earning himself two seconds, as Remo leaped onto the edge and launched himself into a position that allowed him to take out the two guards on each side with a split kick, before swinging his right leg back in to crush the temple of the table-turner.

The remaining one was the smartest of the five, as evidenced by his showing the good sense to run away the moment the carnage began—buying him five yards and a squawk for help into a radio. Remo crouched to the ground and pressed his thumb against one of the scattered playing cards. A quick flick, and the card was embedded in the guard's trachea, blood trickling down the torso of a one-eyed jack.

But the squawk had been enough. Through a set of double doors at the far end of the room rushed a half-dozen more guards. They had the advantage of not being caught unawares, and they were ready for a fight, with their weapons shouldered and ready to fire.

"How many boobs do they have around this place?" Remo marveled. The snow coating his skin now offered him no advantage, so he rejected it and it sloughed off in one fluid movement.

Six machine guns fired, their deafening reports filling the air as bullets perforated the walls.

Six machine guns missed. Then five, four, as Remo slipped between lines of fire, dismantling gun after gun, driving the barrel of each up through the chin of the man who held it.

Three. Two.

As the last body dropped to the floor, the ensuing silence was quickly broken by the sound of slow clapping echoing off the walls. Remo turned and saw two young women—twins—with shoulder-length raven hair framing perfect porcelain faces looking down from a second floor mezzanine.

"Now *these* boobs I recognize," Remo said, taking in the impressive 42D (and 41½ D) orbs that protested being constrained by the buttons of the white cotton blouses the women wore.

"Bravo, Mr. Blomberg," Jackie Forben applauded.

"Ladies," he said, with a slight nod of the head.

Jill Forben giggled. "Oh, I think you know us much better than that, Mr. Blomberg," she said, her mouth drawn up in a coy little grin.

It had been early in Remo's career with CURE that he had encountered Jackie and Jill Forben. Their father, colloquially known as Doctor Quake, had invented a water laser which could, when properly used, release the pressure in natural fault lines and prevent major earthquakes. It could also create major earthquakes as well, and Forben and his daughters had decided the more profitable use of the invention was to extort payments from the U.S. Government in order not to see California crumble into the Pacific.

Remo had been sent out to California under the guise of a department store owner, Remo Blomberg. By the end of that caper, the girls had already murdered several men. The last time Remo saw the girls, they were falling into a crevasse which closed over them, while Chiun was destroying their father's diabolical water-laser that was being used to create localized earthquakes. The second-to-last time he saw them, they had been passed out naked in his bed.

"You left us for dead, Mr. Blomberg," Jackie scolded. "That was very naughty."

"Believe me, I feel just as badly about that as you do," said Remo. "I'm usually much better at leaving people for dead. That was really quite embarrassing."

He had begun to stroll toward the girls. "If you're coming to force us to tell you where the bombs are, it's really unnecessary," Jill said. "We'll be glad to tell you where they are."

"Well, that would be helpful," Remo admitted.

"We'll tell you because you won't stop them," Jackie said. "And we'll have our revenge at last."

"Revenge?" Remo asked. "Blowing up the Earth like

some cartoon Martian is a bit extreme punishment for me leaving you alive, isn't it?"

"If we hadn't been trapped in an air pocket when the fault line sealed over us, we would have died. It was such a tight squeeze!" said Jill.

"Very tight," Jackie giggled.

"It took us hours to claw our way out. Almost a whole day, in fact."

"And when we emerged, we had nothing left." Jackie scowled, her face darkening. "No equipment. Certainly not the money. We were completely on the outs. Homeless."

"We were just lucky to find Billy," said Jill.

"Billy?" Remo asked. He raised an eyebrow quizzically. "You mean, you two and the old man…?"

Jackie rolled her eyes. "No. Not that we didn't offer it, over and over, but Billy insists his heart belongs to Jesus."

"We tried to tell him that wasn't the part we were interested in," added Jill with a titter that sent a distracting jiggle through her breasts. "He blushes so cutely every time we tease him, though, but it's always rejection."

"But we managed," Jackie said. "We get by like we always have." She reached out a hand and Jill's fingers entwined with hers.

"Ah," Remo said.

"You could still kill us, I suppose, but you have a little less than ten minutes before the very big bang," Jackie cooed.

"Eight minutes, thirty-seven seconds," Remo said, still

ticking down the time. "That would still leave plenty of time after showing you two the other thing I'm really good at."

"Really?" Jill asked, her eyebrows raised in a display of innocent astonishment. "Eight minutes to kill us, then go a mile and a half northwest, over that ridge, and deal with the remaining guards between here and there?"

Remo frowned, his brow collapsing down over his deep set eyes. He spun toward the door at a sprint.

"Run, Mr. Blomberg," Jill called out after him. "Run very fast."

• • •

"How's that for fast?" Remo asked, panting. He'd just done the previously unthinkable—he had run the four-minute-mile. "One for the record books."

Chiun shook his head ruefully. "You run like a turtle," he said. "Like a brick. Like a turtle carrying bricks."

"Bullshit," he said, his breath coming back to him. "I was the freaking wind, in case you weren't watching. I just broke records!"

A fingertip flicked out, raising a welt on Remo's forehead.

"Hey!" he cried out. "What did you do that for?"

"What did you tell me before you began this effort?" Chiun asked.

"I don't know. Something like 'Watch my dust?'"

Chiun nodded. "And where did you say this?"

"Back there," Remo said, motioning down the road he had just sprinted in Guinness-impressing time.

BULLY PULPIT

The old Korean smiled. "Exactly," he said. "A mile back, you bragged to me how fast you were going to run. And now here you are, one mile later, telling me how fast you ran."

"Yeah, that's about the size of it, I guess." Remo said. He should have known that nothing he did would ever impress Chiun, but that didn't stop him from trying.

Chiun sat on the ground, his green and black ornate kimono spread out neatly around him. Remo sighed and sat opposite him, assuming the "story time" position.

"In my home of Sinanju," Chiun began, "there were days of great happiness as I continued my training. Often times, I would run along the beautiful beaches, racing my brother. Despite being just a few years my younger, he was swift of foot, and our races were always very close. Sometimes I would reach the goal first, sometimes he would. Those were beautiful days. What have you learned from this?"

Remo closed his eyes and tried to picture two Korean boys running along the coast of the shithole of a dilapidated town. He tried to hear their laughter, the pounding of their feet in the sand. He could smell the salt water of the bay.

He opened his eyes and looked upon the Master of Sinanju.

"Nothing. I learned nothing," he said.

Chiun sagged and sighed and questioned the gods why he had to be the Master saddled with the least observant white man in all of the western world. "The lesson," Chiun said, "is that I am not a twin."

"Oh," said Remo. "I see."

"No, you do not see," Chiun said. "And you did not see." *He stood. "Now, go back. Faster. Break the wind again. I will speak to you further once you are there."*

Remo growled and took off at a sprint. About a quarter of a mile down the road, it dawned on him just how much of an idiot he could be.

• • •

A three-minute-mile was little more than a brisk jog for Remo these days. When he was in a hurry, he could almost halve that. And he *was* in a hurry. Even still, the lack of a paved road, the blowing snow, and the two dozen armed guards who had been radioed to expect him left him just a few seconds over four minutes when he ripped through the metal garage doors of the concrete warehouse storing the bombs.

He was relieved. The whole time he was running, he thought that he was going to have to figure out which one of the bombs was set to go off, but that wasn't going to be an issue.

They were all counting down—all one hundred and ten of them.

Their timers hit 4:00. Remo closed his eyes and let his senses reach out. There was no way anybody went through and set all these bombs to go off by hand. Humans—ordinary humans—weren't that precise; some of them would at least be a second off. Which meant the timers were synched somewhere, some sort of central controller.

Remo opened his eyes and looked left under a cabinet along a far wall and saw what he was looking for, one of the tools of civilization that he hated the most: a computer.

3:45. Remo opened the cabinet and saw a keyboard and a monitor. The monitor displayed a countdown that flashed the same neon green digits replicated across the warehouse on each of the bombs. By now, having seen Avital defuse the bomb in Syria, Remo could have had more than half of the bombs rendered inert. But that wasn't his plan.

The principle Walker was applying, the technique he obviously gleaned from Jackie and Jill Forben, was a simple one. It was a basic tenet of Sinanju, but one that was so simple even American children understood it at a very young age. It was the First Law of Swing Sets. You give a little push, the kid in the swing, no matter how fat, moves forward a little. You give the same push at the height of his backswing, he moves forward a little more. Eventually, the fat kid is swinging out over the playground and pretending he's an astronaut.

But you don't stop a swinging fat kid by no longer pushing him. Oh, that would work, but it would take too long. No, you stopped the swinging fat kid the same way you started him—with a push, but at the wrong time.

3:30. There were arrows beside the counter on the screen, one pointing up, the other pointing down. Remo touched the glass of the screen, tapping the downward-pointing arrowhead. Nothing happened. "That always works when

Smitty does it," he groused. He looked down at the keyboard. Among the many keys, it too had arrows, pointing in all four directions. He stabbed the one with the icon of a downward pointing arrow a few times.

The timer quickly dropped from 3:23 to 3:18.

Perfect, Remo thought, as he began to rapidly tap the key, accelerating the countdown. The timer reached 1:49 and he stopped. Just enough time.

He bolted for the door. This time the only guards he knew he would encounter would be dead ones. He hit the open air with 1:42 seconds to spare. Plenty of time to get as far away as possible and shelter in the deepest snowbank he could find.

In the distance, he heard a helicopter lift off and fly away from his location, and told himself that he made the right choice, even if his new calculations told him he'd have had just about 8 seconds to spare to kill the girls.

With twelve seconds on his internal timer, he ran off the road and into the snow. He prepared to dive beneath the snow when he heard the hammer of God stroke the earth behind him, lighting up the night.

"Still ten seconds off," he chided himself as he let the snow swallow him, this time voluntarily, allowing the heat and debris to pass harmlessly past.

• • •

Fifteen seconds earlier, in a remote cave in the side of a mountain in northern Afghanistan, Achmed had just attached the power cord to his brand new six-year-old PC to replace the one that had been shorted out by the urinating rat.

"Now," he said, "it is time to completely demoralize the American youth with my faster processor."

He flipped up the big red switch at the base of the tower unit, and looked over at the pile of backpack units that were ready to be distributed to his brothers that night for upcoming attacks. He did not register the flash of light as they all detonated at once, disintegrating him and barbecuing the goat copulation going on just outside the entrance to the cave, which did not solely involve goats.

CHAPTER TWENTY-ONE

REMO'S RETURN TO THE COMPOUND was considerably smoother, largely due to the fact that the guards he encountered this time were more hurdles than obstacles, lying dead on the gravel path. He was sure there must be some stragglers somewhere around the facility, but he'd take care of them as he came across them. And he was mad enough to do it slowly, because his true target was miles away now, probably already resting comfortably in the back seat of a little Cessna on his way to God knew where.

So he'd clean up shop here, and worry about Walker and the Forben twins later.

He was right about stragglers. There were more than he expected, beginning right at the fence line. But they were scared. They'd seen too many bodies and no bullet holes. Ripped off limbs, yes. Gouged out eyes, yes. Heads crushed like overripe squash, yes. But no bullet holes. Whatever demon did this to their comrades, they were not eager to meet.

But meet him they did. They didn't know where he was, and they couldn't tell where his path took him. When they heard a scream from the south, they looked that way, only to hear another strangled scream from the north. And with each scream, their numbers dwindled by ones and twos.

Remo was running a clockwise spiral around the facility, working his way in toward the center, toward the two-story warehouse where he'd left a score of dead guards and two girls he should have killed a long time ago. He was meeting less and less resistance, and when he circled his way through the lower level of the main building and began to mount the stairs to the top level, he was pretty sure there weren't any more guards.

That didn't explain the singing, though, that he heard winding its way mournfully down the main hallway on the upper level. One door was slightly ajar, leaking a weak beam of illumination across the hallway.

"And we, who living, yet remain, caught up, shall meet our faithful Lord." The baritone was mostly strong and soulful, but with a hitch in it that came from crying. *"This hope we cherish not in vain."* Remo silently pushed open the door. *"But we comfort one another by this word...*come in, young man. Come in."

Remo came in. The Reverend Billy Walker sat at a metal desk, cleared of everything except a leather Bible worn with years of reading and re-reading. He made no move to either attack or to defend, which was enough to make Remo suspicious.

"There's no one left, is there?" the Reverend asked. He

took a white handkerchief from his breast pocket and wiped his eyes, then his forehead.

"None that I've seen," Remo said flatly.

"And my girls?"

Remo frowned. "Gone." Then he clarified, "Took a copter out."

Walker nodded. "Well, at least there's that," he said softly to himself.

"Guess you got left behind."

"Left behind?" Walker smiled weakly, then laughed. "I was always going to be left behind. That was all part of the grand plan."

Remo studied the man. Old but not decrepit. He wasn't making any threats, wasn't presenting any of the usual aggravation at being defeated. "You're not your usual run of the mill terrorist," Remo said. "You haven't made any demands; you've kept under the radar. What's with all this? What did you have to gain?"

Walker wiped his nose with the handkerchief. "No demands?" he scoffed. "Oh, I made a whopper of a demand." He began to tear up again, and Remo rolled his eyes.

"You know who I am, don't you?" he said to Remo. "What I do."

Remo shrugged. "Some preacher with a plan to blow up the world is all I know."

The Reverend nodded. "I'm in a foolish kind of business," Walker said. "I try to tell people that things can be better, point them to an example of how to live, and show them the promise of Heaven."

"Sounds like a preacher to me," Remo said.

"But I don't do it for money," Walker added. "That's what makes it a foolish kind of business. My only gain is realized beyond this world, and I willingly sacrificed that."

"And this is where you're going to tell me why, right?" Remo sighed. "Go ahead, get it off your chest."

Walker looked directly into Remo's flat, black eyes. Not many people could do that. "Do you believe in God, young man?"

Remo shrugged. "Depends on which one you're asking about."

Walker sagged. "'*The devils also believe, and tremble*,'" he said. "I believe, with all my heart and soul. I believe He lives, I believe He loves us, and...and I believe with all my heart that He's coming back for us one day."

The tears were flowing again, necessitating another wipe with the handkerchief. "I've seen so much in my life," Walker continued. "Seen so many people come to God...only to later leave Him, to fall away and lose their salvation. I couldn't save them."

"People are free to make their own choices," Remo said.

"Ah, but how many people are tempted into the *wrong* choices?" Walker countered. "Why would one willingly give up glory? Even my brethren in the ministry, men and women of God who've done great things, began to fall into the gutters of unrighteousness. Of idolatry. Of prostitution. Of greed. And I knew that if God did not return quickly, very quickly, there would be none left to come back for. *'And except those days should be shortened, there should no flesh be saved: but for the elect's sake those days shall be shortened.'"*

"So, your plan was to kill everybody before anyone who was good had a chance to be bad?"

"Oh no," Walker said shaking his head. "No, I had far more hubris than that. I knew people would die, of course. But I didn't really want to destroy the planet. I just wanted to hold it hostage." He looked up at Remo with red, baleful eyes. "He promised to come back. *He promised!* And if the Earth were going to crumble, then He'd have to come back before that, wouldn't He? *Wouldn't He?*"

Remo stood silent, as the Reverend's body shook with great heaving sobs. He almost felt sorry for the guy. He only killed a bunch of people in what he thought was the greater good. Give him a paycheck for it, and a phone line straight to Smitty, and what would be the difference between the two of them?

"And now I am damned to Hell for all eternity," Walker moaned. "'*For I could wish that myself were accursed from Christ for my brethren, my kinsmen according to the flesh.*' But now? Now it was for nothing. Nothing at all." He lay his head on the desk, both hands cradling the leather book his forehead lay upon.

"Hey," Remo said, interrupting the sobbing. "Hey, chin up. I hear your boss, he's supposed to be real big in the forgiveness business, right? I mean, that's what he does, isn't it?"

Walker looked up, a glimmer of hope in his eyes. "I've

asked Him," Walker croaked. "Every night, even though I knew I was going through with it."

Remo shrugged. "Well, ask him again."

Walker bowed his head and closed his eyes. He murmured a small, private prayer, hands clasped in the traditional way. After a few moments, he whispered, "Amen."

He looked up at Remo. "Do you think He did?"

Remo stood beside the Reverend and put a hand on his shoulder. "Only one way to find out," he said. He flicked his hand, brushing the tips of his fingers against the man's temples, shorting out the nerves in his brain. Walker's body fell back in his leather chair, eyes open toward the sky, jaw slack.

And Remo thought he'd be damned if the man didn't look at peace. "Now, how the hell am I going to get back?" Remo wondered. Then he heard the sound of an approaching motor.

• • •

Uri Kotov threw up over the side of the jeep as Boris weaved around bodies when he could, and drove over them when he had to. Boris's crotch told the urine-soaked tale of how he had barely made it into the guard shack when the test bomb he had set in place went off unexpectedly. But this time, the blast was much louder, preceded by a burst of light and smoke coming from the direction of the storage facility. Uri had been tipping his chair backward as he read, and the rumble of the detonations knocked him to the floor, causing him to catch something delicate in his zipper.

"All our comrades," Uri moaned. "We are lucky not to have been blown up ourselves."

Boris grunted. "Don't be stupid," he scolded the younger man. "Do these men look like they died in explosion?"

Uri looked again at the next cluster they passed, and noticed that while some of them were certainly dismembered, none of them had burns of any kind. "A devil," he said in awe.

"Ignore them," Boris said. "We go see who lives, we get our money, we go home."

Uri silently agreed as the jeep threw gravel back as it took the path into their base camp. Outside the main building, they found a man waving them down with both arms. They stopped.

"Where is everybody?" Uri blurted out.

"Dead," the man said. "They're all dead! They've been killed by a maniac! Do you have enough fuel to get out of here?"

Boris grunted. "What about our money?"

"You can go look for money if you want," the man said. "But what good is it if you're not alive to spend it?"

Uri pointed to the back of the jeep. "We have fuel, and extra fuel," he said, indicating the plastic tanks strapped in there. "Get in."

The man got in.

"Wait," Boris said. "Who are you?"

Remo grabbed them both by the back of their scalps and crushed their heads together into a single object. "You ask too many questions," he said, tossing them out the sides and settling into the driver's seat.

CHAPTER TWENTY-TWO

WHEN REMO BRIBED AVITAL OUT OF JAIL three days later, she swore that she'd never speak to him. She repeated this loudly all the way back to the airport in the helicopter, and continued to tell him all the way back to Jersey. Remo was tempted twice to put her to sleep, but he figured that despite having her best intentions at heart, he probably deserved some of this. Besides, she was nowhere near Chiun's class when it came to verbal punishment, although what she lacked in quality she made up for in quantity.

She did, however, make a good showing of stomping away from him when they landed, while Remo strolled quietly behind her, whistling as though he were not with her. He was sure that one dinner later—with assurances that they both got drunk, that he was captured by the bomb maker, and that it took him this long to get loose and kill him—would assuage her feelings. At least, that was his plan. And if any extra convincing was needed, well, he was prepared to go the extra mile if duty called for it.

His plan worked as expected, although it took an extra two miles and a knock on the door from La Haule's management asking that the exuberance please be toned down just a little.

Keeping Avital in the dark as much as possible was important to the world as much as it was important to Remo. It was a needed diversion from his other duty, which was to sit vigil next to the aging Master of Sinanju. He kept a notepad beside his chair as he watched the news, making little tic marks every time an earthquake was mentioned, notating each with the numerical Richter scale measurement.

He was concerned for a while that his efforts had been applied too late. But, eventually, he noticed that the reports came further apart, with lower intensity. The news people also remarked on this, though with less enthusiasm. The middle-aged reporter, who Remo was certain had played professional softball at some point in her life, reminded her handful of viewers that Mother Earth could just be faking them out, and that they should all continue walking to work and continue to keep their electricity turned off.

When the news shows began to lead off with celebrity sex scandals and sports injuries, burying the earthquake (and related body count) news to third or fourth place, Remo was hopeful. He rested his hand on the withered, skeletal hand of his Master, and bent to kiss his wrinkled forehead. "We're going to make it, Little Father," he said.

"We're going to make what?" a thin reedy voice whispered. "Rice? Rice would be nice."

Remo bolted upright. "You're awake."

"Your observational skills are as paltry as ever," Chiun

remarked. "Otherwise you would have noticed that I have been awake for several minutes now, with my eyes closed. What poisons have you allowed these quacks to pump into the temple which is the body of the Master of Sinanju?"

"Just fluids, Little Father," Remo assured him. "No drugs."

"Enough." The Master of Sinanju reached across and slipped the IV from his vein, pulling off the half-dozen heart monitors in the process. The resulting flat line reading and the high-pitched sine wave note brought the doctor and nurses running from their makeshift quarters down the hall.

"Mister Park, you need to sit back!" the doctor exclaimed, amazed to see Chiun alive, let alone moving. Remo stepped between the two of them and gently pushed the doctor backward—landing his hind quarters onto the floor.

"Sorry, Doc," Remo said. "Believe me, you'd have felt a lot worse if you'd made it all the way to him."

The doctor picked himself ignominiously off the floor, while the two nurses who came with him wisely kept their distance. Dusting himself off, the doctor glared at the two of them, at the dangling wires, at the small trickle of blood trailing down Chiun's arm and already coagulating.

"At least let me examine you," he pleaded.

"Humor the man," Remo said to Chiun. "He put in a lot of work dealing with Smitty not letting him treat you."

Chiun snorted. "Because Emperor Smith employs me, he exhibits the wisdom of royalty. And because he is thus wise, and employs this so-called doctor, who am I to question his wisdom, even if the doctor is white?"

The doctor gave Chiun a cursory once-over, listening to his heart, taking his pulse, and largely just shaking his head.

"I can't believe it," he said. "I've heard of coma victims miraculously coming back to consciousness, but never have they come out without the slightest signs of muscular atrophy or atrial fibrillation!"

Chiun smiled at Remo. "See, perfect health."

"I'd still like you to stay in bed for the next few days," the doctor said. "Just to monitor you for...whatever it is I'm missing."

"Bah," Chiun scoffed. "Always the way with doctors. Does the automobile get better by being driven or by being left to languish in the garage? The body must move to heal fully. We shall leave."

"Well, that's too bad," Remo said. "I guess you won't be needing the present I bought you."

Chiun turned to Remo. "You have bought the Master of Sinanju a present?" he asked. His eyes, normally vellum slits, widened in surprise, an emotion Remo seldom managed to evoke from him. "Perhaps you are finally becoming appreciative of the Master of Sinanju, as well you should after all I have taught you. What is it? Gold? Silver?"

"Silver-ish," Remo said. "At least on one side." He went to the television set, placed on a cabinet facing the foot of Chiun's bed. He opened a cabinet and removed a small cardboard box, which he handed to Chiun.

BULLY PULPIT

Chiun handled the item as though Remo had handed him a fish several days dead. But his expression quickly changed to one of appreciation. He stroked the box gently, as though handling a fragile Faberge egg, and when he looked at Remo, Remo was almost certain there was a tear in his eye.

"Perhaps a few days rest would be good," he said. "For meditation purposes."

"Whatever you say, Little Father," Remo said. He took the box as Chiun offered it back to him, walking it over to the television set.

"Thank you," the doctor whispered to Remo, as he exited the room.

"It's easy if you know how," Remo said with a wink. Then he lifted the lid from the box and removed one of the shiny objects inside, which were indeed, as he had described, silver-ish on one side. A few fumbled buttons, a mumbled curse, and an exhortation from Chiun later, and the television came to life, the screen displaying black and white images of a familiar logo while the speakers played a big band version of a familiar song. The light of the screen glinted off the front of the box, reflected in the metallic letters that also formed the familiar logo: *As the Planet Revolves*: The Complete First Season, Collector's Edition.

"Don't ever do that again, Little Father," Remo said. "It was flat-out embarrassing."

"Hush," Chiun said, sitting up in a lotus position on the hospital bed.

"No, I mean it," Remo said. "No more comas. You don't even nap from now on."

Chiun waved him off dismissively. "I knew you were likely going to make a mess of things," he said. "I could not bear to live to see it. Now be silent and stop ruining an old man's appreciation of the arts."

CHAPTER TWENTY-THREE

THE SOAP OPERA COLLECTION KEPT CHIUN PASSIVE for the next several days. The nurses quickly learned to listen for the closing theme music as their cue for when it was safe to fluff a pillow, offer a glass of water, and do whatever made them feel useful. Chiun began to expect them, and, being Chiun, also began to treat them as personal servants, sending them to make rice, then sending them to re-make it when they got it wrong. When they would get aggravated with him, he would put on his "helpless old man" act that would cajole them into doing whatever it was he wanted, which mostly included changing one finished disc for a new one.

Remo did the math and put in a call to Smitty to order *As the Planet Revolves*: The Complete Second Season, The Collector's Edition, and Smitty in turn placed a call to the show's producers to speed along their production, which involved placing an advance order of a thousand copies of all subsequently planned releases in order to make the venture profitable for the studio. The orders would all be shipped to the Cheerful You Soap Company ("makers of fine bathing, clothing, and dish detergents"), whose sponsorship was exclusive to *As the Planet Revolves* and whose patronage kept the show on the air, and the actors and writers employed, despite the program's abysmal ratings.

The night Chiun was due to reach the last episode, Remo went to say farewell to Avital, who herself had taken a brief leave of absence after assuring her people that the ya Homaar matter had been settled once and for all. To her mild surprise they already knew this, and gave the credit to ya Homaar themselves for being so incompetent in the handling of their bombs.

Remo, in contrast, was far from incompetent in the handling of the explosions that shook her body repeatedly that evening. She had initially planned to make mental notes of the American's techniques, certain she could employ them in the future as part of her job. She had tried this each time she was with Remo, and each time she regained control of her body and her tongue, she found herself clawing at her pillow without the slightest idea of how she ended up that way.

Every two hours, Remo let her recover. They'd sit up in bed, she'd have a drink. He even let her watch television because that's what people did, even though there was nothing worthwhile to watch. He no longer had a need to watch the news, but everyone else was still tuning in to make sure there was going to be a tomorrow. He ruefully knew there were more than a few people who tuned in hoping that things would go back to the disaster movie they had become accustomed to living.

"Looks like the apocalypse has been put on hold until further notice," Remo muttered as the latest talking head segued out of a fifteen second bit about the earthquakes into an interview with an American truck driver who nearly foamed at the mouth as he told the reporter's microphone how he was constitutionally entitled to carry his machine gun and bandolier while shopping for groceries.

Avital clicked off the news. That was another thing he liked about her—she had taste.

"It's funny," she said, sitting up and propping a pillow behind her back. "The earthquakes seemed to subside shortly after all the bombings stopped."

Remo closed his eyes. *Don't think about it*, he thought. *Please don't think about it*. But he knew she would.

"You don't suppose one has anything to do with the other? That it was part of ya Homaar's plan all along?" she asked aloud. "But no, that wouldn't make sense. It's not possible."

Remo could sense the gears turning in her head. Avital was smart, stubborn, and tenacious. She didn't know how to let things go. They were all attractive qualities, even without considering her more physical assets. He knew she didn't believe it now, couldn't believe it now. But eventually she'd find something. And then she'd be obligated to report it. And then it would be in a file somewhere, and someone else would learn about it. And the next time, it might land in the hands of someone who would actually pull it off.

He leaned over and kissed her passionately.

"Mmm, I love how quickly you recover," she smiled, momentarily distracted. Her sharp, dangerous sparkling eyes were taking on that drifting, dreamy quality that comes when the body begins to undergo pleasure.

Remo clasped his palm to the side of her neck and kissed her again, once more lightly massaging an artery that fed the limbic centers of her brain. Much needed oxygen was being held back, and nitrogen narcosis was settling in.

"What are you doing?" she asked, her eyes rolling back in ecstasy.

"Two can keep a secret," Remo whispered sadly, kissing her once more. Then he softly laid her back on the bed and closed her eyes before tucking her body in with the sheet. She looked so serene, so peaceful.

Remo tugged on his chinos and pulled on his shirt. He picked up his shoes and gave Avital's body one last rueful glance.

"That's the biz, sweetheart."

THE END

About the Authors

WARREN MURPHY (1933 – 2015) was born in Jersey City, where he worked in journalism and politics until launching the **Destroyer** series with Richard Sapir in 1971. A screenwriter (*Lethal Weapon II*, *The Eiger Sanction*) as well as a novelist, Murphy's work has won a dozen national awards, including multiple Edgars and Shamuses. He has lectured at many colleges and universities, and is currently offering writing lessons at his website, **WarrenMurphy.com**. A Korean War veteran, some of Murphy's many hobbies included golf, mathematics, opera, and investing. He has served on the board of the Mystery Writers of America, and has been a member of the Screenwriters Guild, the Private Eye Writers of America, the International Association of Crime Writers, and the American Crime Writers League. He has five children: Deirdre, Megan, Brian, Ardath, and Devin.

R.J. Carter is the product of early exposure to American comic books, which he devoured in between sessions of large bowls of sugar-coated cereals and Saturday morning cartoons. Despite this, he still managed to get the girl and have a family, but only because she deluded herself into thinking he would change. He is the author of ALICE'S JOURNEY BEYOND THE MOON, NICHOLAS' CAGE, and A KNIGHT BEFORE CHRISTMAS. He is also the co-author of TIME HUNTER: THE SIDEWAYS DOOR. Most recently, he has contributed the story "Fool's Paradise" to Warren Murphy's *Destroyer* anthology MORE BLOOD.

Find out more about the Destroyer series at www.DestroyerBooks.com, and check out Destroyer Books on Facebook!

Also by Warren Murphy

The DESTROYER Series (with Richard Sapir)
Books 1 – 50:

Created the Destroyer
Death Check
Chinese Puzzle
Mafia Fix
Dr. Quake
Death Therapy
Union Bust
Summit Chase
Murder's Shield
Terror Squad
Kill or Cure
Slave Safari
Acid Rock
Judgment Day
Murder Ward
Oil Slick
Last War Dance
Funny Money
Holy Terror
Assassin's Playoff
Deadly Seeds
Brain Drain
Child's Play
King's Curse
Sweet Dreams

In Enemy Hands
The Last Temple
Ship of Death
The Final Death
Mugger Blood
The Head Men
Killer Chromosomes
Voodoo Die
Chained Reaction
Last Call
Power Play
Bottom Line
Bay City Blast
Missing Link
Dangerous Games
Firing Line
Timber Line
Midnight Man
Balance of Power
Spoils of War
Next of Kin
Dying Space
Profit Motive
Skin Deep
Killing Time

Find out more about the other 100+ titles in the DESTROYER series at DestroyerBooks.com!

The TRACE Series:
Trace
And 47 Miles of Rope
When Elephants Forget
Pigs Get Fat
Once a Mutt
Too Old a Cat
Getting Up With Fleas

The DIGGER Series:
Smoked Out
Fool's Flight
Dead Letter
Lucifer's Weekend

The LEGACY Series (with Gerald Welch):
Forgotten Son
The Killing Fields
Overload
Trial and Terror
Mother Mine

Warren Murphy has written dozens of other books — too many books to list in one place! For more information about the **Destroyer** series (or any of Warren's other books), feel free to write to us at DestroyerBooks@gmail.com. News, information, and updates are posted regularly on DestroyerBooks.com, and make sure to "like" Destroyer Books on Facebook for news, Chiun's words of wisdom, and much more!

I AM BECOME SHIVA, THE DESTROYER; DEATH, THE SHATTERER OF WORLDS

Made in the USA
Coppell, TX
19 July 2020